Letters from England 1846-1849

Elizabeth Davis Bancroft

(Mrs. George Bancroft)

Contents

LETTERS FROM ENGLAND
1846-1849

BY

Elizabeth Davis Bancroft

(Mrs. George Bancroft)

LETTER: TO W.D.B. AND A.B. LIVERPOOL, October 26, 1846

My dear sons: Thank God with me that we are once more on TERRA FIRMA. We arrived yesterday morning at ten o'clock, after a very rough voyage and after riding all night in the Channel in a tremendous gale, so bad that no pilot could reach us to bring us in on Saturday evening. A record of a sea voyage will be only interesting to you who love me, but I must give it to you that you may know what to expect if you ever undertake it; but first, I must sum it all up by saying that of all horrors, of all physical miseries, tortures, and distresses, a sea voyage is the greatest . . . The Liverpool paper this morning, after announcing our arrival says: "The GREAT WESTERn, notwithstanding she encountered throughout a series of most severe gales, accomplished the passage in sixteen days and twelve hours."

To begin at the moment I left New York: I was so absorbed by the pain of parting from you that I was in a state of complete apathy with regard to all about me. I did not sentimentalize about "the receding shores of my country;" I hardly looked at them, indeed. Friday I was awoke in the middle of the night by the roaring of the wind and sea and SUCH motion of the vessel.

The gale lasted all Saturday and Sunday, strong from the North, and as we were in the region where the waters of the Bay of Fundy run out and meet those of the Gulf of St. Lawrence, afterwards we had a strong cross sea. May you never experience a "cross sea." . . . Oh how I wished it had pleased God to plant some little islands as resting-places in the great waste of waters, some resting station. But no, we must keep on, on, with everything in motion that your eye could rest on. Everything tumbling about . . . We lived through it, however, and the sun of Sunday morn rose clear and bright. A pilot got on board about seven and at ten we were in Liverpool.

We are at the Adelphi. Before I had taken off my bonnet Mr. Richard Rathbone, one of the wealthiest merchants here, called to invite us to dine the next day . . . Mrs. Richard Rathbone has written that beautiful "Diary of Lady Willoughby," and, what is more, they say it is a perfect reflect of her own lovely life and character. When she published the book no one knew of it but her husband, not even her brothers and sisters, and, of course, she constantly heard speculations as to the authenticity of the book, and was often appealed to for her opinion. She is very unpretending and sweet in her manners; talks little, and seems not at all like a literary lady.

I like these people in Liverpool. They seem to me to think less of fashion and more of substantial excellence than our wealthy people. I am not sure but the existence of a higher class above them has a favorable effect, by limiting them in some ways. There is much less show of furniture in the houses than with us, though their servants and equipages are in much better keeping. I am not sorry to be detained here for a few days by my illness to become acquainted with them, and I think your father likes it also, and will find it useful to him. Let me say, while I think of it, how much I was pleased with the GREAT WESTERN. That upper saloon with the air passing through it was a great comfort to me. The captain, the servants, the table, are all excellent. Everything on board was as nice as in the best hotel, and my gruels and broths beautifully made. One of the stewardesses did more for me than I ever had done by any servant of my own . . . Your father and Louisa were ill but three or four days, and then your father read Tacitus and talked to the ladies, while Louisa played with the other children.

The Adelphi, my first specimen of an English hotel, is perfectly comfortable, and though an immense establishment, is quiet as a private house. There is none of the bustle of the Astor, and if I ring my bedroom bell it is answered by a woman who attends to me assiduously. The landlord pays us a visit every day to know if we have all we wish.

LONDON, Sunday, November 1

Here I am in the mighty heart, but before I say one word about it I will go on from Wednesday evening with my journal. On Thursday, though still very feeble, I dined at Green Bank, the country-seat of Mr. William Rathbone. I was unwilling to leave Liverpool without sharing with your father some of the hospitalities offered to us and made a great effort to go. The place is very beautiful and the house full of comfortable elegance.

The next morning we started for Birmingham, ninety-seven miles from Liverpool, on our way to London, as I am unable to travel the whole way in a day. On this railway I felt for the first time the superiority of England to our own country. The cars are divided into first, second, and third classes. We took a first-class car, which has all the comforts of a private carriage.

Just as we entered Birmingham I observed the finest seat, surrounded by a park wall and with a very picturesque old church, that I had seen on the way. On enquiring of young Mr. Van Wart, who came to see us in Birmingham (the nephew of Washington Irving), whose place it was, he said it was now called Aston Hall and was owned by Mr. Watt, but it was formerly owned by the Bracebridges, and was the veritable "Bracebridge Hall," and that his uncle had passed his Christmas there.

On arriving here we found our rooms all ready for us at Long's Hotel, kept by Mr. Markwell, a wine merchant. The house is in New Bond Street, in the very centre of movement at the West End, and Mr. Markwell full of personal assiduity, which we never see with us. He comes to the carriage himself, gives me his arm to go upstairs, is so much obliged to us for honoring his house, ushers you in to dinner, at least on the first day, and seats you, etc., etc.

Do not imagine us in fresh, new-looking rooms as we should be in New York or Philadelphia. No, in London even new things look old, but almost everything IS old. Our parlor has three windows down to the floor, but it is very dark. The paint is maple color, and everything is dingy in appearance. The window in my bedroom looks like a horn lantern, so thick is the smoke, and yet everything is scrupulously clean. On our arrival, Boyd, the Secretary of Legation, soon came, and stayed to dine with us at six. Our dinner was an excellent soup, the boiled cod garnished with fried smelts, the roast beef and a FRICANDEAU with sweet breads, then a pheasant, and afterwards, dessert.

This morning Mr. Bates came very early to see us, and then Mr. Joseph Coolidge, who looks very young and handsome; then Mr. Colman, who also looks very well,

Mr. Boyd and a Mr. Haight, of New York, and Mr. Gair, son of Mr. Gair of Liverpool, a pleasing young man.

Monday Evening

This morning came Mr. Aspinwall, then Captain Wormeley, then Dr. Holland, then Mrs. Bates, then Mr. Joseph Jay and his sister, then Tom Appleton, Mrs. and Miss Wormeley, and Mrs. Franklin Dexter. Dr. Holland came a second time to take me a drive, but Mrs. Bates being with me he took your father. Mrs. Bates took me to do some shopping, and to see about some houses. They are very desirous we should be in their neighborhood, in Portland Place, but I have a fancy myself for the new part of town. I have been so used all my life to see things fresh and clean-looking, that I cannot get accustomed to the London dinge, and some of the finest houses look to me as though I would like to give them a good scouring. Tell Cousin M. never to come to England, she would be shocked every minute, with all the grandeur. A new country is cleaner-looking, though it may not be so picturesque.

I got your letters when I arrived here, and I wish this may give you but a little pleasure they gave me. Pray never let a steamer come without a token from both of you . . . With love to Grandma and Uncle Thomas, believe me, with more love than ever before, ELIZABETH D. BANCROFT

LETTER: To W.D.B. and A.B. LONDON, November 3, 1846

. . . This day, at five, your father had his first interview with Lord Palmerston, who will acquaint the Queen with his arrival, and after she has received him we shall leave our cards upon all the ministers and CORPS DIPLOMATIQUE.

November 4th

Your father had a most agreeable dinner at Lord Holland's. He met there Lord and Lady Palmerston, Lord Morpeth, Lord de Mauley, Mr. Harcourt, a son of the Archbishop of York, etc. He took out Lady Holland and Lord Morpeth, Lady Palmerston, the only ladies present. Holland House is surrounded by 200 acres in the midst of the western part of London, or rather Kensington. Lord Holland has no children, and the family dies with him. They dined in the room in which Addison died.

To-day, to my surprise, came Lady Palmerston, which was a great courtesy, as it was my place to make the first visit. She is the sister of Lord Melbourne. Lord de Mauley has also been here. . . . To-day I have been driving through some of the best streets in London, and my ideas of its extent and magnificence are rising fast. The houses are more picturesque than ours, and some of them most noble. The vastness of a great capital like this cannot burst upon one at once. Its effect increases daily. The extent of the Park, surrounded by mansions which look, some of them, like a whole history in themselves, has to-day quite dazzled my imagination.

November 5th

This morning, Thursday, came an invitation to dine with Lord and Lady Palmerston on Saturday. Sir George Grey, another of the ministers, came to see us to-day and Lord Mahon. Your father and I have been all the morning looking at houses, and have nearly concluded upon one in Eaton Square. We find a hotel very expensive, and not very comfortable for us, as your father is very restive without his books about him. Mr. Harcourt also came to see us to- day. I mention as many of the names of our visitors as I can recollect, as it will give you some idea of the composition of English society . . . This moment a large card in an envelope has been brought me, which runs thus: "The Lord Steward has received Her Majesty's commands to invite Mr. Bancroft to dinner at Windsor Castle on Thursday, 12th November, to remain until Friday, 13th." I am glad he will dine there before me, that he may tell me the order of performances.

Friday, November 6th

. . . We had to-day a delightful visit from Rogers, the Poet, who is now quite old, but with a most interesting countenance. He was full of cordiality, and, at parting, as he took my hand, said: "Our acquaintance must become friendship." Mr. Harcourt came again and sat an hour with us, and has introduced your father at the Traveller's Club and the Athenaeum Club. To-night came my new lady's maid, Russell. She dresses hair beautifully, but is rather too great a person to suit my fancy.

Sunday Evening, November 8th

On Friday evening we met at Mrs. Wormeley's a cosy little knot of Americans. The Dexters were staying there and there were Mr. and Mrs. Atkinson and Miss Pratt, Mr. and Mrs. Aspinwall, Mr. and Miss Jay, Mr. and Mrs. Putnam, Mr. Colman, Mr. Pickering, etc.

Wednesday Evening

On Monday we came to our HOME, preferring it to the hotel, though it is not yet in order for our reception, and we have not yet all our servants. Last evening we dined with Lord Morpeth at his father's house. His family are all out of town, but he remains because of his ministerial duties. Lord Morpeth took me out and I sat between him and Sir George Grey. Your father took out Lady Theresa Lewis, who is a sister of Lord Clarendon. She was full of intelligence and I like her extremely. Baron and Lady Parke (a distinguished judge), Lady Morgan, Mr. Mackintosh, Dr. and Mrs. Holland (Sidney Smith's daughter), and Mr. and Mrs. Franklin Dexter, with several others were the party.

During dinner one gentleman was so very agreeable that I wondered who he could be, but as Lord Palmerston had told me that Mr. Macaulay was in Edinburgh,

I did not think of him. After the ladies left the gentlemen, my first question to Mrs. Holland was the name of her next neighbor. "Why, Mr. Macaulay," was her answer, and I was pleased not to have been disappointed in a person of whom I had heard so much. When the gentlemen came in I was introduced to him and talked to him and heard him talk not a little.

These persons all came the next day to see us, which gave rise to fresh invitations.

This morning we have been driving round to leave cards on the CORPS DIPLO-MATIQUE, and Mr. Harcourt has taken me all over the Athenaeum Club-house, a superb establishment. They have given your father an invitation to the Club, a privilege which is sometimes sought for years, Mr. Harcourt says. . . . Have I not needed all my energies? We have been here just a fortnight, and I came so ill that I could hardly walk. We are now at housekeeping, and I am in the full career in London society. They told me I should see no one until spring, but you see we dine out or go out in the evening almost every day. . . . For the gratification of S.D. or Aunt I., who may wonder how I get along in dress matters, going out as I did in my plain black dress, I will tell you that Mrs. Murray, the Queen's dressmaker, made me, as soon as I found these calls and invitations pouring in, two dresses. One of black velvet, very low, with short sleeves, and another of very rich black watered silk, with drapery of black tulle on the corsage and sleeves. . . . I have fitted myself with several pretty little head-dresses, some in silver, some with plumes, but all white, and I find my velvet and silk suit all occasions. I do not like dining with bare arms and neck, but I must.

Tuesday, November 17th

Last evening we passed at the Earl of Auckland's, the head of the Admiralty. The party was at the Admiralty, where there is a beautiful residence for the first lord. . . . I had a long talk with Lord Morpeth last evening about Mr. Sumner, and told him of his nomination. He has a strong regard for him. . . . Not a moment have I had to a London "lion." I have driven past Westminster, but have not been in it. I have seen nothing of London but what came in my way in returning visits.

LETTER: To I.P.D. LONDON, November 17, 1846

My dear Uncle: I cannot help refreshing the remembrance of me with you and dear Aunty by addressing a separate letter to you. . . . Yesterday we hailed with delight our letters from home. . . . One feels in a foreign land the absence of common sympathies and interests, which always surround us in any part of our own country. And yet nothing can exceed the kindness with which we have been received here.

Last evening I went to my first great English dinner and it was a most agreeable one. . . . It seems a little odd to a republican woman to find herself in right of her country taking precedence of marchionesses, but one soon gets used to all things. We sat down to dinner at eight and got through about ten. When the ladies rose, I found I was expected to go first. After dinner other guests were invited and to the first person who came in, about half-past ten, Lady Palmerston said: "Oh, thank you for coming so early." This was Lady Tankerville of the old French family of de Grammont and niece to Prince Polignac. The next was Lady Emily de Burgh, the daughter of the Marchioness of Clanricarde, a beautiful girl of seventeen. She is very lovely, wears a Grecian braid round her head like a coronet, and always sits by her mother, which would not suit our young girls. Then came Lord and Lady Ashley, Lord Ebrington, and so many titled personages that I cannot remember half.

The dinner is much the same as ours in all its modes of serving, but they have soles and turbot, instead of our fishes, and their pheasants are not our pheasants, or their partridges our partridges. Neither have we so many footmen with liveries of all colours, or so much gold and silver plate. . . . The next morning Mr. Bancroft breakfasted with Dr. Holland to meet the Marquis of Lansdowne alone. [Thursday] he went down to Windsor to dine with the Queen. He took out to dinner the

Queen's mother, the Duchess of Kent, the Queen going with the Prince of Saxe-Weimar, who was paying a visit at the Castle. He talked German to the Duchess during dinner, which I suspect she liked, for the Queen spoke of it to him afterwards, and Lord Palmerston told me the Duchess said he spoke very pure German. While he was dining at Windsor I went to a party all alone at the Countess Grey's, which I thought required some courage.

Of all the persons I see here the Marquis of Lansdowne excites the most lively regard. His countenance and manners are full of benevolence and I think he understands America better than anyone else of the high aristocracy. I told him I was born at Plymouth and was as proud of my pure Anglo-Saxon Pilgrim descent as if it were traced from a line of Norman Conquerors. Nearly all the ministers and their wives came to see us immediately, without waiting for us to make the first visit, which is the rule, and almost every person whom we have met in society, which certainly indicates an amiable feeling toward our country. We could not well have received more courtesy than we have done, and it has been extended freely and immediately, without waiting for the forms of etiquette. Pray say to Mr. Everett how often we hear persons speak of him, and with highest regard. I feel as if we were reaping some of the fruits of his sowing.

Mr. Bancroft sends you a pack of cards, one of the identical two packs with which the Queen played Patience the evening he was at Windsor. They were the perquisite of a page who brought them to him. He was much pleased with the Queen and thought her much prettier than any representation of her which we have seen, and with a very sweet expression. Lady Holland had been staying two or three days at Windsor, and was to leave the next morning. When the Queen took leave of her at night, she kissed her quite in my Virginia fashion.

Dear Uncle: How much more your niece would have written if to-day were not packet day, I cannot say. I shall send you some newspapers and a pack of cards which I saw in the Queen's hands. The American Minister and Mrs. Bancroft have since played a game of piquet with them. The Queen's hands were as clean as her smile was gracious. Best regards to the Judge and Aunt Isaac.

Yours most truly, George Bancroft.

LETTER: To W.D.B. and A.B. LONDON, November 29, 1846

After a long interval I find again a quiet Sunday evening to resume my journal to you. On Monday we dined at Lord John Russell's, and met many of the persons we have met before and the Duchess of Inverness, the widow of the Duke of Sussex. On Tuesday we dined at Dr. Holland's. His wife and daughter are charming, and then we met, besides, Lady Charlotte Lindsay, the only surviving child of Lord North, Mr. and Mrs. Milman (the author of the "Fall of Jerusalem"), and Mr. Macaulay. Yesterday I went to return the visit of the Milmans and found that the entrance to their house, he being a prebend of Westminster Abbey, was actually in the cloisters of the Abbey. They were not at home, but I took my footman and wandered at leisure through the cloisters, treading at every step on the tomb of some old abbot with dates of 1160 and thereabouts.

Nothing could be more delightful than London is now, if I had only a little more physical vigor to enjoy it. We see everybody more frequently, and know them better than in the full season, and we have some of the best specimens of English society, too, here just now, as the Whig ministry brings a good deal of the ability of the aristocracy to its aid. The subjects of conversation among women are more general than with us, and [they] are much more cultivated than our women as a body, not our blues. They never sew, or attend, as we do, to domestic affairs, and so live for social life and understand it better.

LONDON, December 2, 1846

My dear Mrs. Polk: you told me when I parted from you at Washington that you would like to get from me occasionally some accounts of my experiences in English society. I thought at that time that we should see very little of it until the spring, but contrary to my expectation we have been out almost every day since our arrival. We made our DEBUT in London on the first day of November (the suicidal month you know) in the midst of an orange-colored fog, in which you could not see your hand before you. The prospect for the winter seemed, I must say, rather "triste," but the next day the fog cleared off, people came constantly to see us, and we had agreeable invitations for every day, and London put on a new aspect. Out first dinner was at Lord Palmerston's, where we met what the newspapers call a distinguished circle. The Marquis of Lansdowne, Lord and Lady John Russell, Marquis and Marchioness of Clanricarde (Canning's daughter), Earl and Countess Grey, Sir George and Lady Grey, etc., etc. I was taken out by Lord Palmerston, with Lord Grey on the other side, and found the whole thing very like one of our Washington dinners, and I was quite as much at my ease, and they seemed made of the same materials as our cabinet at home. I have since dined at Lord Morpeth's, Lord John Russell's, Lord Mahon's, Dr. Holland's, Baron Parke's, The Prussian Minister's, and to-day we dine with the Duchess of Inverness, the widow of the Duke of Sussex; to-morrow with Mr. Milman, a prebend of Westminster and a distinguished man of letters. We have been at a great many SOIREES, at Lady Palmerston's, Lady Grey's, Lord Auckland's, Lady Lewis's, etc., etc.

And now, having given you some idea WHOM we are seeing here, you will wish to know how I like them, and how they differ from our own people. At the smaller dinners and SOIREES at this season I cannot, of course, receive a full impression of English society, but certainly those persons now in town are charming people. Their manners are perfectly simple and I entirely forget, except when their historic names fall upon my ear, that I am with the proud aristocracy of England. All the persons whose names I have mentioned to you give one a decided impression not only of ability and agreeable manners, but of excellence and the domestic virtues. The furniture and houses, too, are less splendid and ostentatious, than those of our large cities, though [they] have more plate, and liveried servants. The forms of society and the standard of dress, too, are very like ours, except that a duchess or a countess has more hereditary point lace and diamonds. The general style of dress, perhaps, is not so tasteful, so simply elegant as ours. Upon the whole I think more highly of our own country (I mean from a social point of view alone) than before I came abroad. There is less superiority over us in manners and all the social arts than I could have believed possible in a country where a large and wealthy class have been set apart from time immemorial to create, as it were, a social standard of high refinement. The chief difference that I perceive is this: In our country the position of everybody is undefined and rests altogether upon public opinion. This leads sometimes to a little assumption and pretension of manner, which the highest class here, whose claims are always allowed by all about them, are never tempted to put on. From this results an extreme simplicity of manner, like that of a family circle among us.

What I have said, however, applies less to the South than to the large cities of the North, with which I am most familiar at home. I hope our memory will not be completely effaced in Washington, for we cling to our friends there with strong interest. Present my respectful regards to the President, and my love to Mrs. Walker and Miss Rucker. To the Masons also, and our old colleagues all, and pray lay your royal commands upon somebody to write me. I long to know what is going on in Washington. The Pleasantons promised to do so, and Annie Payne, to whom and to Mrs. Madison give also my best love. Believe me yours with the highest regard.

E.D. BANCROFT.

LETTER: 2 December

Yesterday we dined at the Prussian Minister's, Chevalier Bunsen's. He met your father in Rome twenty years since, and has received us with great enthusiasm. Yesterday at dinner he actually rose in his seat and made quite a speech welcoming him to England as historian, old friend, etc., and ended by offering his health, which your father replied to shortly, in a few words. Imagine such an outbreak upon routine at a dinner in England! Nobody could have done it but one of German blood, but I dare say the Everetts, who know him, could imagine it all.

LETTER: To W.D.B. and A.B. LONDON, December 19,1846

My dear Sons: . . . Yesterday we dined at Macready's and met quite a new, and to us, a most agreeable circle. There was Carlyle, who talked all dinner-time in his broad Scotch, in the most inimitable way. He is full of wit, and happened to get upon James I., upon which topic he was superb. Then there was Babbage, the great mathematician, Fonblanc, the editor of the EXAMINER, etc., etc. The day before we dined at Mr. Frederick Elliott's with a small party of eight, of which Lady Morgan was one, and also a brother of Lord Normanby's, whom I liked very much. Lady Morgan, who had not hitherto much pleased me, came out in this small circle with all her Irish wit and humor, and gave me quite new notions of her talent. She made me laugh till I cried. On Saturday we dined at Sir Roderick Murchison's, the President of the Geological Society, very great in the scientific way.

We have struck up a great friendship with Miss Murray, the Queen's Maid of Honor, who paid me a visit of three hours to-day, in the midst of which came in Colonel Estcourt, whom I was delighted to see, as you may suppose. Miss Murray is to me a very interesting person, though a great talker; a convenient fault to a stranger. She is connected with half the noble families in England, is the granddaughter of the Duchess of Athol, who governed the Isle of Man as a queen, and the descendant of Scott's Countess of Derby. Though sprung of such Tory blood, and a maid of honor, she thinks freely upon all subjects. Religion, politics, and persons, she decides upon for herself, and has as many benevolent schemes as old Madam Jackson.

I returned the visit of Mr. and Mrs. Leslie, the painter, this week, and saw the picture he is now painting for the Vice-Chancellor. It is a sketch of children, a boy driving his two little sisters as horses. One of the little girls is very like Susie, her size, hair, and complexion. How I longed to be rich enough to order a copy, but his pictures cost a fortune. I paid also a visit this week to the Duchess of Inverness, whom I found in the prettiest, cosiest morning boudoir looking onto the gardens of the Palace. In short, I do, or see, every hour, something that if I were a traveller only, I could make quite a story of.

LETTER: To W.D.B. and A.B. LONDON, January 1, 1847

My dear Sons: . . . I wrote my last sheet on the 19th and your father went on that day to Cambridge to be present at the tri- centennial celebration of Trinity College . . . He went also the day after the anniversary, which was on our 22nd December, to Ely, with Peacock, the great mathematician, who is Dean of Ely, to see the great cathedral there . . . While he was at Cambridge I passed the evening of the 22nd at Lady Morgan's, who happened to have a most agreeable set . . . Lady Morgan's reunions are entertaining to me because they are collections of lions, but they are not strictly and exclusively fashionable. They remind me in their composition from various circles of Mrs. Otis's parties in Boston. We have in this respect an advantage over the English themselves, as in our position we see a great variety of cliques.

For instance, last evening, the 31st, I took Louisa, at half-past seven, to the house of Mr. Hawes, an under Secretary of State, to see a beautiful children's masque. It was an impersonation of the "Old Year" dressed a little like LEAR with snowy hair and draperies. OLD YEAR played his part inimitably, at times with great pathos, and then introducing witty hits at all the doings of his reign, such as exploding cotton, the new planet, a subject which he put at rest as "FAR BEYOND OUR REACH," etc., etc. He then introduced one by one the children of all ages as "Days" of the coming year. There was TWELFTH DAY, crowned as Queen with her cake in her hands; there was CHRISTMAS, covered with holly and mistletoe; there was APRIL FOOL'S DAY, dressed as Harlequin; there was, above all, SHROVE TUESDAY, with her frying-pan of pancakes, dressed as a little cook; there was a charming boy of fourteen or fifteen, as ST. VALENTINE'S DAY with his packet of valentines addressed to the young ladies present; there was the 5TH OF NOVEMBER, full of wit and fun, etc.; the longest day, an elder brother, of William's height, with a cap of three or four feet high; and his little sister of five, as the shortest day. This was all arranged to music and each made little speeches, introducing themselves. The OLD YEAR, after introducing his successors, and after much pathos, is "going, going--gone," and falls covered with his drapery, upon removing which, instead of the lifeless body of the OLD YEAR, is discovered a sweet little flower- crowned girl of five or six, as the NEW YEAR. It was charming, and I was so pleased that, instead of taking Louisa away at nine o'clock as I intended, I left her to see "Sir Roger de Coverly," in the dress of his time. Last night at Mr. Putnam's, I met William and Mary Howitt, and some of the lesser lights. I have put down my pen to answer a note, just brought in, to dine next Thursday with the Dowager Countess of Charleville, where we were last week, in the evening. She is eighty-four (tell this to Grandmamma) and likes still to surround herself with BEAUX and BELLES ESPRITS, and as her son and daughter reside with her, this is still easy . . . The old lady talks French as fast as possible, and troubles me somewhat by talking it to me, forgetting that a foreign minister's wife can talk English . . . Your father likes to be here. He has copying going on in the State Paper Office and British Museum, and his heart is full of manuscripts. It is the first thought, I believe, whoever he sees, what papers are in their family. He makes great interest with even the ladies sometimes for this purpose. Upon the whole, I love my own country better than ever, but whether I shall not miss, upon my return, some things to which I am gradually getting accustomed, I have yet to learn. The gratification of mixing constantly with those foremost in the world for rank, science, literature, or all which adorns society is great, but there is a certain yearning toward those whose habits, education, and modes of thought are the same as our own, which I never can get over. In the full tide of conversation I often stop and think, "I may unconsciously be jarring the prejudices or preconceived notions of these people upon a thousand points; for how differently have I been trained from these women of high rank, and men, too, with whom I am now thrown." Upon all topics we are accustomed to think, perhaps, with more latitude, religion, politics, morals, everything. I like the English extremely, even more than I expected, and yet happy am I to think that our own best portions of society can bear a comparison with theirs. When I see you I can explain to you the differences, but I think we need not be ashamed of ourselves.

LETTER: To I.P.D. LONDON,
January 2, 1847

My dear Uncle: . . . I refer you to my letters to my boys, for all the new persons and places we may have seen lately, while I give you for Aunty's amusement a minute account of my visit into the country at Mr. Bates's, where things are managed in a scrupulously English manner, so that it will give her the same idea of country life here, as if it were a nobleman's castle. Our invitation was to arrive on Thursday, the day before Christmas, to dine, and to remain until the following Tuesday morning. His place is at East SHEEN, which receives its name from the Anglo-Saxon word for BEAUTY. It adjoins Richmond Park, beyond which is the celebrated Richmond Hill, Twickenham, Kew, etc., etc. . . . We arrived at East Sheen at half- past five; but I ought first to mention the PREPARATIONS for a country excursion. Our own carriage has, of course, no dickey for my maid, or conveniences for luggage, so we take a travelling carriage. The imperials (which are large, flat boxes, covering the whole top of the carriage, CAPITAL for velvet dresses, and smaller ones fitting into all the seats IN the carriage, and BEFORE and BEHIND) are brought to you the day before. I am merely asked what dresses I wish taken, and that is all I know of the matter, so thoroughly does an English maid understand her business. We were shown on our arrival into a charming room, semi-library.

In a few minutes a servant came to show me to my apartment, which was very superb, with a comfortable dressing-room and fire for Mr. Bancroft, where the faithful Keats unpacked his dressing materials, while I was in a few moments seated at the toilet to undergo my hair-dressing, surrounded by all my apparatus, and a blazing fire to welcome me with a hissing tea-kettle of hot water and every comfort. How well the English understand it, I learn more and more every day. My maid had a large room above me, also with a fire; indeed, a "lady's" maid is a VERY GREAT character INDEED, and would be much more unwilling to take her tea with, or speak familiarly to, a footman or a housemaid than I should. My greatest mistakes in England have been committed toward those high dignitaries, my own maid and the butler, whose grandeur I entirely misappreciated and invaded, as in my ignorance I placed them, as we do, on the same level with other servants. She has her fire made for her, and LOAF sugar in her tea, which she and Cates sip in solitary majesty. However, she is most conscientious and worthy, as well as dignified, and thoroughly accomplished in her business. As all these things are pictures of English life, I mention them to amuse Aunty, who likes to know how these matters are managed.

After I am dressed, I join the circle in the library, where I am introduced to Mr. and Madam Van de Weyer, and Louis Buonaparte, the son of Louis, the ex-King of Holland, and of Hortense, Josephine's daughter. He was a long time imprisoned in the fortress of Ham, and has not long been free. There was also Napoleon, son of Jerome Buonaparte, and the Princess of Wurtemberg. They were most agreeable, intelligent, and amiable young men, and I was glad to meet them. Lord and Lady Langdale (who have a place in the neighborhood) were invited to dine with us. He is Master of the Rolls and was elevated to the peerage from great distinction at the bar. Lady Langdale is a sensible and excellent person. At dinner I sat between Mr. Bates and Lord Langdale, whom I liked very much.

The next morning we assembled at ten for breakfast, which was at a round table, with a sort of circular tray, which turns at the least touch in the centre, leaving only a rim round the table for plates and cups. This was covered also with a white cloth and on it were placed all the breakfast viands, with butter, sugar, cream, bread, toast-rack and preserves. You need no servants, but turn it round and help yourself. I believe the Van de Weyers introduced it, from a visit in Wales. Tea and coffee are served from a side-table always, here. Let me tell Aunty that our simple breakfast DRESS is unknown in England. You come down in the morning dressed for the day, until six or seven in the evening, when your dress is low neck and short sleeves for dinner. At this season the morning dress is a rich silk or velvet, high body quite close in the throat with handsome collar and cuffs, and ALWAYS a cap. Madam Van de Weyer wore every day a different dress, all very rich, but I adhered to a black watered silk with the same simple cap I wore at home.

I took a drive through Richmond Park (where Henry the Eighth watched to see a signal on the Tower when Anne Boleyn's head fell, and galloped off to marry Jane Seymour) to Richmond Terrace, which is ravishingly beautiful even at this season. . . . The next day the gentleman all went to town, and Madam Van de Weyer and I passed the day TETE-A-TETE, very pleasantly, as her experience in diplomatic life is very useful to me. . . . Her manners are very pleasing and entirely unaffected. She has great tact and quickness of perception, great intelligence and amiability and is altogether extremely well-fitted for the ROLE she plays in life. Her husband is charming. . . . They have three children, very lovely. The eldest, Victor, a fine boy of seven years old, Victoria, a girl of four, for whom the Queen was sponsor, and Albert, to whom Prince Albert performed the same office. This was, of course, voluntary in the royal parties, as it was not a favor to be asked. . . . Madam Van de Weyer is not spoiled, certainly, by the prominent part she was called to play in this great centre of the world at so early an age, and makes an excellent courtier. I could not help pitying her, however, for looking forward to going through, year after year, the same round of ceremonies, forms, and society. For us, it is a new study, and invaluable for a short time; but I could not bear it for life, as these European diplomatists. Besides, we Americans really enjoy a kind of society, and a much nearer intercourse than other foreigners, in the literary, scientific, and even social circles.

On Saturday evening Lord William Fitzroy and daughter joined our party with Sir William Hooker and Lady Hooker. . . . Sir William Hooker is one of the most interesting persons I have seen in England. He is a great naturalist and has the charge of the great Botanical Gardens at Kew. He devoted a morning to us there, and it was the most delightful one I have passed. There are twenty-eight different conservatories filled with the vegetable wonders of the whole world. Length of time and regal wealth have conspired to make the Kew gardens beyond our conceptions entirely. . . . Sir William pointed out to us all that was very rare or curious, which added much to my pleasure. . . . He showed us a drawing of the largest FLOWER ever known on earth, which Sir Stamford Raffles discovered in Sumatra. It was a parasite without leaves or stem, and the flower weighed fifteen pounds. Lady Raffles furnished him the materials for the drawing. I dined in company with her not long ago, and regret now that I did not make her tell me about the wonders of that region. At the same dinner you may meet so many people, each having their peculiar gift, that one cannot avail oneself of the opportunity of extracting from each what is precious. I always wish I could sit by everybody at the same time, and I could often employ a dozen heads, if I had them, instead of my poor, miserable one. From Sir William Hooker I learned as much about the VEGETABLE world, as Mr. Bancroft did from the Dean of Ely on ARCHITECTURE, when he expounded to him the cathedral of Ely; pointing out the successive styles of the Gothic, and the different periods in which the different parts were built. Books are dull teachers compared with these gifted men giving you a lecture upon subjects before your eyes.

On Sunday we dined with out own party; on Monday some diplomatic people, the Lisboas and one of Mr. Bates's partners, and on Tuesday we came home. I must not omit a visit while we were there from Mr. Taylor (Van Artevelde), who is son-in-law of Lord Monteagle, and lives in the neighborhood. He has a fine countenance and still finer voice, and is altogether one of those literary persons who do not disappoint you, but whose whole being is equal to their works. I hope to see more of him, as they spoke of "CULTIVATING" us, and Mr. Taylor was quite a PROTEGE of our kind and dear friend, Dr. Holland, and dedicated his last poem to him. This expression, "I shall CULTIVATE you," we hear constantly, and it strikes me as oddly as our Western "BEING RAISED." Indeed, I hear improper Anglicisms constantly, and they have nearly as many as we have. The upper classes, here, however, do SPEAK English so roundly and fully, giving every LETTER its due, that it pleases my ear amazingly.

On Wednesday I go for the first time to Westminster Abbey, on Epiphany, to hear the Athanasian Creed chanted. I have as yet had no time for sight-seeing, as the days are so short that necessary visits take all my time. No one goes out in a carriage till after two, as the servants dine at one, and in the morning early the footman is employed in the house. A coachman never leaves his box here, and a footman is indispensable on all occasions. No visit can be paid till three; and this gives me very little time in these short days. Everything here is inflexible as the laws of the Medes and Persians, and though I am called "Mistress" even by old Cates with his grey hair and black coat, I cannot make one of them do anything, except BY the person and AT the time which English custom prescribes. They are brought up to fill certain situations, and fill them perfectly, but cannot or will not vary.

I am frequently asked by the ladies here if I have formed a household to please me and I am obliged to confess that I have a very nice household, but that I am the only refractory member of it. I am always asking the wrong person for coals, etc., etc. The division of labor, or rather ceremonies, between the butler and footman, I have now mastered I believe in some degree, but that between the UPPER and UNDER house-maid is still a profound mystery to me, though the upper has explained to me for the twentieth time that she did only "the top of the work." My cook comes up to me every morning for orders, and always drops the deepest curtsey, but then I doubt if her hands are ever profaned by touching a poker, and she NEVER washes a dish. She is cook and HOUSEKEEPER, and presides over the housekeeper's room; which has a Brussels carpet and centre table, with one side entirely occupied by the linen presses, of which my maid (my vice-regent, only MUCH greater than me) keeps the key and dispenses every towel, even for the kitchen. She keeps lists of everything and would feel bound to replace anything missing. I shall make you laugh and Mrs. Goodwin stare, by some of my housekeeping stories, the next evening I pass in your little pleasant parlor (a word unknown here).

LETTER: To W.D.B. and A.B. LONDON,
January 10, 1847

My very dear Children: . . . Yesterday we dined at Lady Charleville's, the old lady of eighty-four, at whose house I mentioned an evening visit in my last, and I must tell you all about it to entertain dear Grandma. I will be minute for once, and give you the LITTLE details of a London dinner, and they are all precisely alike. We arrived at Cavendish Square a quarter before seven (very early) and were shown into a semi-library on the same floor with the dining-room. The servants take your cloak, etc., in the passage, and I am never shown into a room with a mirror as with us, and never into a chamber or bedroom.

We found Lady Charleville and her daughter with one young gentleman with whom I chatted till dinner, and who, I found, was Sir William Burdette, son of Sir Francis and brother of Miss Angelina Coutts. I happened to have on the corsage of my black velvet a white moss rose and buds, which I thought rather youthful for ME, but the old lady had [them] on her cap. She is full of intelligence, and has always been in the habit of drawing a great deal. . . . Very soon came in Lord Aylmer, [who] was formerly Governor of Canada, and Lady Colchester, daughter of Lord Ellenborough, a very pretty woman of thirty-five, I should think; Sir William and Lady Chatterton and Mr. Algernon Greville, whose grandmother wrote the beautiful "Prayer for Indifference," an old favorite of mine, and Mr. MacGregor, the political economist. Lord Aylmer took me out and I found him a nice old peer, and discovered that ever since the death of his uncle, Lord Whitworth, whose title is extinct, he had borne the arms of both Aylmer and Whitworth. Mr. Bancroft took out Lady Colchester, and the old lady was wheeled out precisely as Grandma is.

At table she helped to the fish (cod, garnished round with smelts) and insisted on carving the turkey herself, which she did extremely well. By the way, I observe they never carve the breast of a turkey LONGITUDINALLY, as we do, but in short slices, a little diagonally from the centre. This makes many more slices, and quite large enough where there are so many other dishes. The four ENTREE dishes are always placed on the table when we sit down, according to our old fashion, and not one by one. They have [them] warmed with hot water, so that they keep hot while the soup and fish are eaten. Turkey, even BOILED turkey, is brought on AFTER the ENTREES, mutton (a saddle always) or venison, with a pheasant or partridges. With the roast is always put on the SWEETS, as they are called, as the term dessert seems restricted to the last course of fruits. During the dinner there are always long strips of damask all round the table which are removed before the dessert is put on, and there is no brushing of crumbs. You may not care for all this, but the house-keepers may. I had Mr. Greville the other side of me, who seemed much surprised that I, an American, should know the "Prayer for Indifference," which he doubted if twenty persons in England read in these modern days.

It is a great mystery to me yet how people get to know each other in London. Persons talk to you whom you do not know, for no one is introduced, as a general rule. I have sometimes quite an acquaintance with a person, and exchange visits, and yet do not succeed for a long time in putting their name and the person together. . . . It is a great puzzle to a stranger, but has its conveniences for the English themselves. We are endeavoring to become acquainted with the English mind, not only through society, but through its products in other ways. Natural science is the department into which they seem to have thrown their intellect most effectively for the last ten or fifteen years. We are reading Whewell's "History of the Inductive Sciences," which gives one a summary of what has been accomplished in that way, not only in past ages, but in the present. Every moment here is precious to me and I am anxious to make the best use of it, but I have immense demands on my time in every way.

LETTER: To W.D.B. and A.B. Tuesday night, January 19, 1847

To-day we have been present at the opening of Parliament, but how can I picture to you the interest and magnificence of the scene. I will begin quite back, and give you all the preparations for a "Court Day." Ten days before, a note was written to Lord Willoughby d'Eresby, informing him of my intention to attend, that a seat might be reserved for me, and also soliciting several tickets for American ladies and gentlemen. . . . I cannot take them with me, however, as the seat assigned to the ladies of Foreign Ministers is very near the throne. This morning when I awoke the fog was thicker than I ever knew it, even here. The air was one dense orange-colored mass. What a pity the English cannot borrow our bright blue skies in which to exhibit their royal pageants!

Mr. Bancroft's court dress had not been sent home, our servants' liveries had not made their appearance, and our carriage only arrived last night, and I had not passed judgment upon it. Fogs and tradesmen! these are the torments of London. Very soon came the tailor with embroidered dress, sword, and chapeau, but, alas! Mr. Isidore, who was to have dressed my hair at half-past ten was not forthcoming, and to complete my perplexity, he had my head-dress in his possession. At last, just as Russell had resumed her office at the toilet, came Isidore, a little before twelve, coiffure and all, which was so pretty that I quire forgave him all his sins. It was of green leaves and white FLEUR-DE-LIS, with a white ostrich feather drooping on one side. I wear my hair now plain in front, and the wreath was very flat and classical in its style. My dress was black velvet with a very rich bertha. A bouquet on the front of FLEUR-DE- LIS, like the coiffure, and a Cashmere shawl, completed my array. I have had the diamond pin and earrings which you father gave me, re-set, and made into a magnificent brooch, and so arranged that I can also wear it as a necklace or bracelet. On this occasion it was my necklace.

Miss Murray came to go with me, as she wished to be by my side to point out everybody, and her badge as Maid of Honor would take her to any part of the house. At half-past twelve she and I set out, and after leaving us the carriage returned for your father and Mr. Brodhead. But first let me tell you something of our equipage. It is a CHARIOT, not a coach; that is, it has but one seat, but the whole front being glass makes it much more agreeable to such persons as have not large families. The color is maroon, with a silver moulding, and has the American arms on the panel. The liveries are blue and red; on Court Days they have blue plush breeches, and white silk stockings, with buckles on their shoes. Your father leaves all these matters to me, and they have given me no little plague. When I thought I had arranged everything necessary, the coachman, good old Brooks, solicited an audience a day or two ago, and began, "Mistress, did you tell them to send the pads and the fronts and the hand-pieces?" "Heavens and earth! what are all these things?" said I. "Why, ma'am, we always has pads under the saddle on Court Days, trimmed round with the colors of the livery, and we has fronts made of ribbin for the horses' heads, and we has white hand-pieces for the reins." This is a specimen of the little troubles of court life, but it has its compensations. To go back to Miss Murray and myself, who are driving through the park between files of people, thousands and thousands all awaiting with patient, loyal faces the passage of the Queen and of the State carriages. The Queen's was drawn by eight cream-colored horses, and the servants flaming with scarlet and gold. This part of the park, near the palace, is only accessible to the carriages of the foreign ministers, ministers, and officers of the household.

We arrive at the Parliament House, move through the long corridor and give up our tickets at the door of the chamber. It is a very long, narrow room. At the upper end is the throne, on the right is the seat of the ambassadors, on the left, of their ladies. Just in front of the throne is the wool-sack of the Lord Chancellor, looking like a drawing-room divan, covered with crimson velvet. Below this are rows of seats for the judges, who are all in their wigs and scarlet robes; the bishops and the peers, all in robes of scarlet and ermine. Opposite the throne at the lower end is the Bar of the Commons. On the right of the Queen's chair is a vacant one, on which is carved the three plumes, the insignia of the Prince of Wales, who will occupy it when he is seven or nine years old; on the left Prince Albert sits.

The seat assigned me was in the front row, and quite open, like a sofa, so that I could talk with any gentleman whom I knew. Madam Van de Weyer was on one side of me and the Princess Callimachi on the other, and Miss Murray just behind me. She insisted on introducing to me all her noble relatives. Her cousin, the young Duke of Athol; the Duke of Buccleuch; her nephew the Marquis of Camden; her brother the Bishop of Rochester. There were many whom I had seen before, so that the hour passed very agreeably. Very soon came in the Duke of Cambridge, at which everybody rose, he being a royal duke. He was dressed in the scarlet kingly robe, trimmed with ermine, and with his white hair and whiskers (he is an old man) was most picturesque and scenic, reminding me of King Lear and other stage kings. He requested to be introduced to me, upon which I rose, of course. He soon said, "Be seated," and we went on with the conversation. I told him how much I liked Kew Garden, where he has a favorite place.

When I first entered I was greeted very cordially by a personage in a black gown and wig, whom I did not know. He laughed and said: "I am Mr. Senior, whom you saw only Saturday evening, but you do not know me in my wig." It is, indeed, an entire transformation, for it reaches down on the shoulders. He is a master in chancery. He stood by me nearly all the time and pointed out many of the judges, and some persons not in Miss Murray's line.

But the trumpets sound! the Queen approaches! The trumpet continues, and first enter at a side door close at my elbow the college of heralds richly dressed, slowly, two and two; then the great officers of the household, then the Lord Chancellor bearing the purse, seal, and speech of the Queen, with the macebearers before him. Then Lord Lansdowne with the crown, the Earl of Zetland, with the cap of maintenance, and the Duke off Wellington, with the sword of State. Then Prince Albert, leading the Queen, followed by the Duchess of Sutherland, Mistress of the Robes, and the Marchioness of Douro, daughter-in-law of the Duke of Wellington, who is one of the ladies in waiting. The Queen and Prince sit down, while everybody else remains standing. The Queen then says in a voice most clear and sweet: "My lords (rolling the r), be seated." Upon which the peers sit down, except those who enter with the Queen, who group themselves about the throne in the most picturesque manner. The Queen had a crown of diamonds, with splendid necklace and stomacher of the same. The Duchess of Sutherland close by her side with her ducal coronet of diamonds, and a little back, Lady Douro, also, with her coronet. On the right of the throne stood the Lord Chancellor, with scarlet robe and flowing wig, holding the speech, surrounded by the emblems of his office; a little farther, one step lower down, Lord Lansdowne, holding the crown on a crimson velvet cushion, and on the left the Duke of Wellington, brandishing the sword of State in the air, with the Earl of Zetland by his side. The Queen's train of royal purple, or rather deep crimson, was borne by many train-bearers. The whole scene seemed to me like a dream or a vision. After a few minutes the Lord Chancellor came forward and presented the speech to the Queen. She read it sitting and most exquisitely. Her voice is flute-like and her whole emphasis decided and intelligent. Very soon after the speech is finished she leaves the House, and we all follow, as soon as we can get our carriages.

Lord Lansdowne told me before she came in that the speech would be longer than usual, "but not so long as your President's speeches." It has been a day of high pleasure and more like a romance than a reality to me, and being in the very midst of it as I was, made it more striking than if I had looked on from a distant gallery.

LETTER: To W.D.B. and A.B. LONDON, February 7, 1847

My dear Sons: . . . On Friday we dined with two bachelors, Mr. Peabody and Mr. Coates, who are American bankers. Mr. Peabody is a friend of Mr. Corcoran and was formerly a partner of Mr. Riggs in Baltimore. Mr. Coates is of Boston. . . . They mustered up all the Americans that could be found, and we dined with twenty-six of our countrymen.

Monday Morning

Last evening we were at home to see any Americans who might chance to come. . . . I make tea in the drawing-room, on a little table with a white cloth, which would not be esteemed COMME IL FAUT with us. There is none of the parade of eating in the largest evening party here. I see nothing but tea, and sometimes find an informal refreshment table in the room where we put on our cloaks.

I got a note yesterday from the O'Connor Don, enclosing an order to admit me to the House of Commons on Monday. . . . You will be curious to know who is "The O'Connor Don." He is Dennis O'Connor, Esq., but is of the oldest family in Ireland, and the representative of the last kings of Connaught. He is called altogether the O'Connor Don, and begins his note to me with that title. You remember Campbell's poem of "O'Connor's Child"?

Sunday, 14th February

. . . Yesterday morning was my breakfast at Sir Robert Inglis's. The hour was halfpast nine, and as his house is two miles off I had to be up wondrous early for me. The weather has been very cold for this climate for the last few days, though we should think it moderate. They know nothing of extreme cold here. But, to return to or breakfast, where, notwithstanding the cold, the guests were punctually assembled: The Marquis of Northampton and his sisters, the Bishop of London with his black apron, Sir Stratford Canning, Mr. Rutherford, Lord Advocate for Scotland, the Solicitor-General and one or two others. The conversation was very agreeable and I enjoyed my first specimen of an English breakfast exceedingly. . . . Our invitations jostle each other, now Parliament has begun, for everybody invites on Wednesday, Saturday, or Sunday, when there are no debates. We had three dinner invitations for next Wednesday, from Mr. Harcourt, Marquis of Anglesey, and Mrs. Mansfield. We go to the former. The Queen held a levee on Friday, for gentlemen only. Your father went, of course.

Sunday, February 21st

I left off on Sunday, on which day I got a note from Lady Morgan, saying that she wished us to come and meet some agreeables at her house. . . . There I met Sir William and Lady Molesworth, Sir Benjamin Hall, etc., and had a long talk with "Eothen," who is a quiet, unobtrusive person in manner, though his book is quite an effervescence. . . . On Wednesday we dined with Mr. Harcourt, and met there Lord Brougham, who did the talking chiefly, Lord and Lady Mahon, Mr. Labouchere, etc. It was a most agreeable party, and we were very glad to meet Lord Brougham, whom we had not before seen.

Lord Brougham is entertaining, and very much listened to. Indeed, the English habit seems to be to suffer a few people to do up a great part of the talking, such as Macaulay, Brougham, and Sydney Smith and Mackintosh in their day. . . . On Saturday evening, at ten o'clock, we went to a little party at Lady Stratheden's. After staying there three-quarters of an hour we went to Lady Palmerston's, where were all the GREAT London world, the Duchess of Sutherland among the number. She is most noble, and at the same time lovely. . . . We had an autograph note from Sir Robert Peel, inviting us to dine next Saturday, and were engaged. I hope they will ask us again, for I know few things better than to see him, as we should in dining there. I have the same interest in seeing the really distinguished men of England, that I should have in the pictures and statues of Rome, and indeed, much greater. I wish I was better prepared for my life here by a more extensive culture; mere fine ladyism will not do, or prosy bluism, but one needs for a thorough enjoyment of society, a healthy, practical, and extensive culture, and a use of the modern languages in our position would be convenient. I do not know how a gentleman can get on without it here, and I find it so desirable that I devote a good deal of time to speaking French with Louisa's governess. Your father uses French a great deal with his colleagues, who, many of them, speak English with great difficulty, and some not at all. . . . Lady Charlotte Lindsay came one day this week to engage us to dine with her on Wednesday, but yesterday she came to say that she wanted Lord Brougham to meet us, and he could not come till Friday. Fortunately we had no dinner engagement on that day, and we are to meet also the Miss Berrys; Horace Walpole's Miss Berrys, who with Lady Charlotte herself, are the last remnants of the old school here.

LETTER: To I.P.D. February 21st

My dear Uncle: . . . I wrote [J.D.] a week or two before I heard of his death, but was unable to tell him anything of Lord North, as I had not met Lady Charlotte Lindsay. I have seen her twice this week at Baron Parke's and at Lord Campbell's, and told her how much I had wished to do so before, and on what account. She says her father heard reading with great pleasure, and that one of her sisters could read the classics: Latin and, I think, Greek, which he enjoyed to the last. She says that he never complained of losing his sight, but that her mother has told her that it worried him in his old age that he remained Minister during our troubles at a period when he wished, himself, to resign. He sometimes talked of it in the solitude of sleepless nights, her mother has told her.

On Tuesday morning we were invited by Dr. Buckland, the Dean of Westminster, to go to his house, and from thence to the Abbey, to witness the funeral of the Duke of Northumberland. The Dean, who has control of everything in the Abbey, issued tickets to several hundred persons to go and witness the funeral, but only Lord Northampton's family, the Bunsens (the Prussian Minister), and ourselves, went to his house, and into the Dean's little gallery.

After the ceremony there were a crowd of visitors at the Dean's, and I met many old acquaintances, and made many new ones, among whom were Lady Chantrey, a nice person. After the crowd cleared off, we sat down to a long table at lunch, always an important meal here, and afterward the Dean took me on his arm and showed me everything within the Abbey precincts. He took us first to the Percy Chapel to see the vault of the Percys. . . . From thence the Dean took us to the Jerusalem chamber where Henry IV died, then all over the Westminster school. We first went to the hall where the young men were eating their dinner. . . . We then went to the school-room, where every inch of the wall and benches is covered with names, some of them most illustrious, as Dryden's. There were two bunches of rods, which the Dean assured me were not mere symbols of power, but were daily used, as, indeed, the broken twigs scattered upon the floor plainly showed. Our ferules are thought rather barbarous, but a gentle touch from a slender twig not at all so. These young men looked to me as old as our collegians. We then went to their study- rooms, play-rooms, and sleeping-rooms. The whole forty sleep in one long and well-ventilated room, the walls of which were also covered with names. At the foot of each bed was a large chest covered with leather, as mouldering and time-worn as the Abbey itself. Here are educated the sons of some of the noblest families, and the Archbishop of York has had six sons here, and all of them were in succession the Captain of the school. . . .

On Wednesday evening we went first to our friends, the Bunsens, where we were invited to meet the Duchess of Sutherland with a few other persons. Bunsen is very popular here. He is learned and accomplished, and was so much praised in the Biography of Dr. Arnold, the late historian of Rome, that he has great reputation in the world of letters. . . . Although we have great pleasure in the society of Chevalier and Madam Bunsen, and in those whom we meet at their house. On this occasion we only stayed half an hour, which I passed in talking with the Bishop of Norwich and his wife, Mrs. Stanley, and went to Lady Morgan's without waiting till the Duchess of Sutherland came. There we found her little rooms full of agreeable people. . . . The next day, Thursday, there was a grand opera for the benefit of the Irish, and all the Diplomatic Corps were obliged to take boxes. Lady Palmerston, who was one of the three patronesses, secured a very good box for us, directly opposite the Queen, and only three from the stage.

We took with us Mrs. Milman and W.T. Davis, to whom it gave a grand opportunity of seeing the Queen and the assembled aristocracy, at least all who are now in London. "God save the Queen," sung with the whole audience standing, was a noble sight. The Queen also stood, and at the end gave three curtsies. On Friday Captain and Mrs. Wormeley, with Miss Wormeley, dined with us, with Mr. and Mrs. Carlyle, Miss Murray, the Maid of Honor, Mr. and Mrs. Pell of New York, with William T. and Mr. Brodhead. William was very glad to see Carlyle, who showed himself off to perfection, uttering his paradoxes in broad Scotch.

Last evening we dined at Mr. Thomas Baring's, and a most agreeable dinner it was. The company consisted of twelve persons, Lord and Lady Ashburton, etc. I like Lady Ashburton extremely. She is full of intelligence, reads everything, talks most agreeably, and still loves America. She is by no means one of those who abjure their country. I have seen few persons in England whom I should esteem a more delightful friend or companion than Lady Ashburton, and I do not know why, but I had received a different impression of her. Lord Ashburton, by whom I sat at dinner, struck me as still one of the wisest men I have seen in England. Lady Ashburton, who was sitting by Mr. Bancroft, leant forward and said to her husband, "WE can bring bushels of corn this year to England." "Who do you mean by WE?" said he. "Why, we Americans, to be sure."

Monday Evening

Yesterday we dined at Count St. Aulair's, the French Ambassador, who is a charming old man of the old French school, at a sort of amicable dinner given to Lord and Lady Palmerston. Lord John Russell was of the party, with the Russian Ambassador and lady, Mr. and Madam Van de Weyer, the Prussian and Turkish Ministers. The house of the French Embassy is fine, but these formal grand dinners are not so charming as the small ones. The present state of feeling between Lord Palmerston and the French Government gave it a kind of interest, however, and it certainly went off in a much better spirit than Lady Normanby's famous party, which Guizot would not attend. It seems very odd to me to be in the midst of these European affairs, which I have all my life looked upon from so great a distance.

LETTER: To Mrs. W.W. Story LONDON, March 23, 1847

My dear Mrs. Story: I should have thanked you by the last steamer for your note and the charming volume which accompanied it, but my thoughts and feelings were so much occupied by the sad tidings I heard from my own family that I wrote to no one out of it. The poems, which would at all times have given me great pleasure, gave me still more here than they would if I were with you on the other side of the Atlantic. I am not cosmopolitan enough to love any nature so well as our American nature, and in addition to the charm of its poetry, every piece brought up to me the scenes amidst which it had been written. . . . How dear these associations are your husband will soon know when he too is separated from his native shores and from those he loves. . . . I shall look forward with great pleasure to seeing him here, and only wish you were to accompany him, for your own sake, for his, and for ours. His various culture will enable him to enjoy most fully all that Europe can yield him in every department. My own regret ever since I have been here has been that the seed has not "fallen upon better ground," for though I thought myself not ignorant wholly, I certainly lose much that I might enjoy more keenly if I were better prepared for it. I envy the pleasure which Mr. Story will receive from music, painting, and sculpture in Europe, even if he were destitute of the creative inspiration which he will take with him. For ourselves, we have everything to make us happy here, and I should be quite so, if I could forget that I had a country and children with very dear friends 3,000 miles away. . . . There are certain sympathies of country which one cannot overcome. On the other hand I certainly enjoy pleasures of the highest kind, and am every day floated like one in a dream into the midst of persons and scenes that make my life seem more like a drama than a reality. Nothing is more unreal than the actual presence of persons of whom one has heard much, and long wished to see. One day I find myself at dinner by the side of Sir Robert Peel, another by Lord John Russell, or at Lord Lansdowne's table, with Mrs. Norton, or at a charming breakfast with Mr. Rogers, surrounded by pictures and marbles, or with tall feathers and a long train, making curtsies to a queen.

LETTER: To W.D.B. and A.B. LONDON, April 2 [1847]

Here it is the day before the despatches leave and I have not written a single line to you. . . . On Friday we dined at Lady Charlotte Lindsay's, where were Lord Brougham and Lady Mallet, Mr. Rogers and the Bishop of Norwich and his wife. In the evening Miss Agnes Berry, who never goes out now, came on purpose to appoint an evening to go and see her sister, who is the one that Horace Walpole wished to marry, and to whom so many of his later letters are addressed. She is eighty-four, her sister a few years younger, and Lady Charlotte not much their junior.

These remnants of the BELLES-ESPRITS of the last age are charming to me. They have a vast and long experience of the best social circles, with native wit, and constant practice in the conversation of society. . . . On Wednesday, we dined at Sir Robert Peel's, with whom I was more charmed than with anybody I have seen yet. I sat between him and the Speaker of the House of Commons. I was told that he was stiff and stately in his manners, but did not think him so, and am inclined to imagine that free from the burden of the Premiership, he unbends more. He talked constantly with me, and in speaking of a certain picture said, "When you come to Drayton Manor I shall show it to you." I should like to go there, but to see himself even more than his pictures. Lady Peel is still a very handsome woman.

The next morning we breakfasted with Mr. Rogers. He lives, as you probably know, in [a] beautiful house, though small, whose rooms look upon the Green Park, and filled with pictures and marbles. We stayed an hour or more after the other guests, listening to his stores of literary anecdote and pleasant talk. In the evening we went to the Miss Berrys', where we found Lord Morpeth, who is much attached to them. Miss Berry put her hand on his head, which is getting a little gray, and said: "Ah, George, and I remember the day you were born, your grandmother brought you and put you in my arms." Now this grandmother of Lord Morpeth's was the celebrated Duchess of Devonshire, who electioneered for Fox, and he led her to tell me all about her. "Eothen" was also there, Lady Lewis and many of my friends. . . . Aunty wishes to know who is "Eothen." She has probably read his book, "Eothen, or Traces of Travel," which was very popular two or three years since. He is a young lawyer, Mr. Kinglake, the most modest, unassuming person in his manners, very shy and altogether very unlike the dashing, spirited young Englishman I figured to myself, whom nothing could daunt from the Arab even to the plague, which he defied.

LETTER: To I.P.D.

Dear Uncle and Aunt: On Thursday [the 25th] we were invited to Sir John Pakington's, whose wife is the Bishop of Rochester's daughter, but were engaged to Mr. Senior, who had asked us to meet the Archbishop of Dublin, the celebrated Dr. Whately. He had come over from Ireland to make a speech in the House of Lords upon the Irish Poor Law. He is full of learning [and] simplicity, and with most genial hearty manners. Rogers was also there and said more fine things than I have heard him say before at dinner, as he is now so deaf that he does not hear general conversation, and cannot tell where to send his shaft, which is always pointed. He retains all his sarcasm and epigrammatic point, but he shines now especially at breakfast, where he has his audience to himself.

We went from Mr. Senior's to Mr. Milman's, but nearly all the guests there were departed or departing, though one or two returned with us to the drawing-room to stay the few minutes we did. Among the lingerers we found Sir William and Lady Duff Gordon, the two Warburtons, "Hochelaga" and "Crescent and Cross," and "Eothen." Mrs. Milman I really love, and we see much of them.

On Saturday was the dreaded Drawing-Room, on which occasion I was to be presented to the Queen. . . . Mr. Bancroft and I left home at a quarter past one. On our arrival we passed through one or two corridors, lined by attendants with battle-axes and picturesque costumes, looking very much like the supernumeraries on the stage, and were ushered into the ante-room, a large and splendid room, where only the Ministers and Privy Councillors, with their families, are allowed to go with the Diplomatic Corps. Here we found Lady Palmerston, who showed me a list she had got Sir Edward Cust, the master of ceremonies, to make out of the order of precedence of the Diplomatic Corps, and when the turn would come for us who were to be newly presented. The room soon filled up and it was like a pleasant party, only more amusing, as the costumes of both gentlemen and ladies were so splendid. I got a seat in the window with Madam Van de Weyer and saw the Queen's train drive up. At the end of this room are two doors: at the left hand everybody enters the next apartment where the Queen and her suite stand, and after going round the circle, come out at the right-hand door. After those who are privileged to go FIRST into the ANTE-ROOM leave it, the general circle pass in, and they also go in and out the same doors. But to go back. The left-hand door opens and Sir Edward Cust leads in the Countess Dietrichstein, who is the eldest Ambassadress, as the Countess St. Aulair is in Paris. As she enters she drops her train and the gentlemen ushers open it out like a peacock's tail. Then Madam Van de Weyer, who comes next, follows close upon the train of the former, then Baroness Brunnow, the Madam Bunsen, then Madam Lisboa, then Lady Palmerston, who, as the wife of the Minister for Foreign Affairs, is to introduce the Princess Callimachi, Baroness de Beust, and myself. She stations herself by the side of the Queen and names us as we pass. The Queen spoke to none of us, but gave me a very gracious smile, and when Mr. Bancroft came by, she said: "I am very glad to have had the pleasure of seeing Mrs. Bancroft to- day." I was not [at] all frightened and gathered up my train with as much self-possession as if I were alone. I found it very entertaining afterward to watch the reception of the others. The Diplomatic Corps remain through the whole, the ladies standing on the left of the Queen and the gentlemen in the centre, but all others pass out immediately. . . . On Sunday evening Mr. Bancroft set off for Paris to pass the Easter recess of Parliament. . . . I got a very interesting letter yesterday from Mr. Bancroft. It seems that the Countess Circourt, whose husband has reviewed his book and Prescott's, is a most charming person, and makes her house one of the most brilliant and attractive in Paris. Since he left, a note came from Mr. Hallam, the contents of which pleased me as they will you. It announced that Mr. Bancroft was chosen an Honorary Member of the Society of Antiquaries, of which Lord Mahon is president, Hallam, vice-president. Hallam says the society is very old and that he is the first citizen of the United States upon whom it has been conferred, but that he will not long possess it exclusively, as his "highly distinguished countryman, Mr. Prescott, has also been proposed."

LETTER: To W.D.B. and A.B.

Tuesday

My dear Sons: . . . On Monday morning came the dear Miss Berrys, to beg me to come that evening to join their circle. They have always the best people in London about them, young as well as old.

The old and the middle-aged are more attended to here than with us, where the young are all in all. As Hayward said to me the other evening, "it takes time to make PEOPLE, like cathedrals," and Mr. Rogers and Miss Berry could not have been what they are now, forty years ago. A long life of experience in the midst constantly of the highest and most cultivated circles, and with several generations of distinguished men gives what can be acquired in no other way. Mr. Rogers said to me one day: "I have learnt more from men that from BOOKS, and when I used to be in the society of Fox and other great men of that period, and they would sometimes say 'I have always thought so and so,' then I have opened my ears and listened, for I said to myself, now I shall get at the treasured results of the experience of these great men." This little saying of Mr. Rogers expresses precisely my own feelings in the society of the venerable and distinguished here. With us society is left more to the crudities of the young than in England. The young may be interesting and promise much, but they are still CRUDE. The elements, however fine, are not yet completely assimilated and brought to that more perfect tone which comes later in life.

Monday, April 12th

. . . On Saturday I went with Sir William and Lady Molesworth to their box in the new Covent Garden opera, which has been opened for the first time this week. There I saw Grisi and Alboni and Tamburini in the "Semiramide." It was a new world of delight to me. Grisi, so statuesque and so graceful, delights the eye, the ear, and the soul. She is sculpture, poetry, and music at the same time. . . . Mr. Bancroft has been received with great cordiality in Paris. He has been three times invited to the Palace, and Guizot and Mignet give him access to all that he wants in the archives, and he passes his evenings with all the eminent men and beautiful women of Paris. Guizot, Thiers, Lamartine, Cousin, Salvandi, Thierry, he sees, and enjoys all. They take him to the salons, too, of the Faubourg St. Germain, among the old French aristocracy, and to innumerable receptions.

Wednesday

To-morrow I go to the Drawing-Room alone, and to complete the climax, the Queen has sent us an invitation to dine at the Palace to-morrow, and I must go ALONE for the FIRST TIME. If I live through it, I will tell you all about it; but is it not awkward in the extreme?

Friday Morning

At eight o'clock in the evening I drove to the Palace. My dress was my currant-colored or grosseille velvet with a wreath of white Arum lilies woven into a kind of turban, with green leave and bouquet to match, on the bertha of Brussels lace. I was received by a servant, who escorted me through a long narrow corridor the length of Winthrop Place and consigned me to another who escorted me in his turn, through another wider corridor to the foot of a flight of stairs which I ascended and found another servant, who took my cloak and showed me into the grand corridor or picture gallery; a noble apartment of interminable length; and surrounded by pictures of the best masters. General Bowles, the Master of the Household, came forward to meet me, and Lord Byron, who is one of the Lords in Waiting. I found Madam Lisboa already arrived, and soon came in Lord and Lady Palmerston, the Duke of Norfolk, the Marquis and Marchioness of Exeter, Lord and Lady Dalhousie, Lord Charles Wellesley, son of the Duke of Wellington, Lady Byron, and Mr. Hallam. We sat and talked as at any other place, when at last the Queen was announced. The gentlemen ranged themselves on one side, and we on the other, and the Queen and Prince passed through, she bowing, and we profoundly curtseying. As soon as she passed the Marquis of Exeter came over and took Madam Lisboa, and Lord Dalhousie came and took me. The Queen and Prince sat in the middle of a long table, and I was just opposite the Prince, between Lord Exeter and Lord Dalhousie, who is the son of the former Governor of Nova Scotia, was in the last ministry, and a most agreeable person. I talked to my neighbors as at any other dinner, but the Queen spoke to no one but Prince Albert, with a word or two to the Duke of Norfolk, who was on her right, and is the first peer of the realm.

The dinner was rather quickly despatched, and when the Queen rose we followed her back into the corridor. She walked to the fire and stood some minutes, and then advanced to me and enquired about Mr. Bancroft, his visit to Paris, if he had been there before, etc. I expressed, of course, the regret he would feel at losing the honor of dining with Her Majesty, etc. She then had a talk with Lady Palmerston, who stood by my side, then with all the other ladies in succession, until at last Prince Albert came out, soon followed by the other gentlemen. The Prince then spoke to all the ladies, as she had done, while she went in succession to all the gentlemen guests. This took some time and we were obliged to stand all the while.

At last the Queen, accompanied by her Lady in Waiting, Lady Mount Edgcumbe, went to a sofa at the other end of the corridor in front of which was a round table surrounded by arm-chairs. When the Queen was seated Lady Mount Edgcumbe came to us and requested us to take our seats round the table. This was a little prim, for I did not know exactly how much I might talk to others in the immediate presence of the Queen, and everybody seemed a little constrained. She spoke to us all, and very soon such of the gentlemen as were allowed by their rank, joined us at the round table. Lord Dalhousie came again to my side and I had as pleasant a conversation with him, rather SOTTO VOCE, however, as I could have had at a private house. At half-past ten the Queen rose and shook hands with each lady; we curtsied profoundly, and she and the Prince departed. We then bade each other good-night, and found our carriages as soon as we chose.

LETTER: To W.D.B. and A.B. LONDON,
May 16, 1847

My dear Sons: My letters by this steamer will have very little interest for you, as, from being in complete retirement, I have no new things to related to you. . . . We have taken advantage of our leisure to drive a little into the country, and on Tuesday I had a pleasure of the highest order in driving down to Esher and passing a quiet day with Lady Byron, the widow of the poet. She is an intimate friend of Miss Murray, who has long wished us to see her and desired her to name the day for our visit.

Esher is a little village about sixteen miles from London, and Lady Byron has selected it as her residence, though her estates are in Leicestershire, because it is near Lord and Lady Lovelace, her only child, the "ADA" of poetry. We went in our own carriage, taking Miss Murray with us, and as the country is now radiant with blossoms and glowing green, the drive itself was very agreeable. We arrived at two o'clock, and found only Lady Byron, with the second boy of Lady Lovelace and his tutor. Lady Byron is now about fifty-five, and with the remains of an attractive, if not brilliant beauty. She has extremely delicate features, and very pale and finely delicate skin. A tone of voice and manner of the most trembling refinement, with a culture and strong intellect, almost masculine, but which betrays itself under such sweet and gentle and unobtrusive forms that one is only led to perceive it by slow degrees. She is the most modest and unostentatious person one can well conceive. She lives simply, and the chief of her large income (you know she was the rich Miss Milbank) she devotes to others. After lunch she wished me to see a little of the country round Esher and ordered her ponies and small carriage for herself and me, while Mr. Bancroft and Miss Murray walked. We went first to the royal seat, Claremont, where the Princess Charlotte lived so happily with Leopold, and where she died. Its park adjoins Lady Byron's, and the Queen allows her a private key that she may enjoy its exquisite grounds. Here we left the pedestrians, while Lady Byron took me a more extensive drive, as she wished to show me some of the heaths in the neighborhood, which are covered with furze, now one mass of yellow bloom.

Every object is seen in full relief against the sky, and a figure on horseback is peculiarly striking. I am always reminded of the beginning of one of James's novels, which is usually, you know, after this manner: "It was toward the close of a dull autumn day that two horsemen were seen," etc., etc. Lady Byron took me to the estate of a neighboring gentleman, to show me a fine old tower covered with ivy, where Wolsey took refuge from his persecutors, with his faithful follower, Cromwell.

Upon our return we found the last of the old harpers, blind, and with a genuine old Irish harp, and after hearing his national melodies for half an hour, taking a cup of coffee, and enjoying a little more of Lady Byron's conversation, we departed, having had a day heaped up with the richest and best enjoyments. I could not help thinking, as I was walking up and down the beautiful paths of Claremont Park, with the fresh spring air blowing about me, the primroses, daisies, and wild bluebells under my feet, and Lady Byron at my side, that it was more like a page out of a poem than a reality.

On Sunday night any Americans who are here come to see us. . . . Mr. Harding brought with him a gentleman, whom he introduced as Mr. Alison. Mr. Bancroft asked him if he were related to Archdeacon Alison, who wrote the "Essay on Taste." "I am his son," said he. "Ah, then, you are the brother of the historian?" said Mr. Bancroft. "I am the historian," was the reply. . . . An evening visitor is a thing unheard of, and therefore my life is very lonely, now I do not go into society. I see no one except Sunday evenings, and, occasionally, a friend before dinner.

LETTER: To W.D.B. and A.B. LONDON, May 24, [1847]

My dear Sons: . . . On Friday we both went to see the Palace of Hampton Court with my dear, good, Miss Murray, Mr. Winthrop and son, and Louise. . . . On our arrival, we found, to our great vexation, that Friday was the only day in the week in which visitors were not admitted, and that we must content ourselves with seeing the grounds and go back without a glimpse of its noble galleries of pictures. Fortunately for us, Miss Murray had several friends among the persons to whom the Queen has assigned apartments in the vast edifice, and they willingly yielded their approbation of our admission if she could possibly win over Mrs. Grundy, the housekeeper. This name sounded rather inauspicious, but Mr. Winthrop suggested that there might be a "Felix" to qualify it, and so in this case it turned out. Mrs. Grundy asserted that such a thing had never been done, that it was a very dangerous precedent, etc., but in the end the weight of a Maid of Honor and a Foreign Minister prevailed, and we saw everything to much greater advantage than if we had 150 persons following on, as Mr. Winthrop says he had the other day at Windsor Castle. . . . On our way [home] we met Lady Byron with her pretty little carriage and ponies. She alighted and we did the same, and had quite a pleasant little interview in the dusty road.

Sunday, May 30th

Your father left town on Monday. . . . He did not return until the 27th, the morning of the Queen's Birthday Drawing-Room. On that occasion I went dressed in white mourning. . . . It was a petticoat of white crape flounced to the waist with the edges notched. A train of white glace trimmed with a ruche of white crape. A wreath and bouquet of white lilacs, without any green, as green is not used in mourning. The array of diamonds on this occasion was magnificent in the highest degree, and everybody was in their most splendid array. The next evening there was a concert at the Palace, at which Jenny Lind, Grisi, Alboni, Mario, and Tamburini sang. I went dressed in [a] deep black dress and enjoyed the music highly. Seats were placed in rows in the concert-room and one sat quietly as if in church. At the end of the first part, the royal family with their royal guests, the Grand Duke Constantine of Russia, and the Grand Duke and Duchess of Saxe-Weimar went to the grand dining-room and supped by themselves, with their suites, while another elegant refreshment table was spread in another apartment for the other guests. . . . Jenny Lind a little disappointed me, I must confess, but they tell me that her songs were not adapted on that evening to the display of her voice.

On Sunday evening your father dined with Baron Brunnow, the Russian Minister, to meet the Grand Duke Constantine. It so happened that the Grand Duke and Duchess of Saxe-Weimar appointed an audience to Baron and Baroness Brunnow at seven, and they had not returned at half-past seven, when the Grand Duke and their other guests arrived. The Baroness immediately advanced to the Grand Duke and sunk on her knees before him, asking pardon in Russian. He begged her to rise, but she remained in the attitude of deep humiliation, until the Grand Duke sunk also on HIS knees and gently raised her, and then kissed her on the cheek, a privilege, you know, of royalty.

. . . On Monday evening we both went to a concert at Mr. Hudson's, the great railway "king," who has just made an immense fortune from railway stocks, and is now desirous to get into society. These things are managed in a curious way here. A NOUVEAU RICHE gets several ladies of fashion to patronize their entertainment and invite all the guests. Our invitation was from Lady Parke, who wrote me two notes about it, saying that she would be happy to meet me at Mrs. Hudson's splendid mansion, where would be the best music and society of London; and, true enough, there was the Duke of Wellington and all the world. Lady Parke stood at the entrance of the splendid suite of rooms to receive the guests and introduce them to their host and hostess. On Tuesday morning I got a note from Mr. Eliot Warburton (brother of "Hochelaga") to come to his room at two o'clock and look at some drawings. To our surprise we found quite a party seated at lunch, and a collection of many agreeable persons and some lions and lionesses. There was Lord Ross, the great astronomer; Baroness Rothschild, a lovely Jewess; Miss Strickland, the authoress of the "Queens of England"; "Eothen," and many more. Mr. Polk, CHARGE at Naples, and brother of the President, dined with us, and Miss Murray, and in the evening came Mr. and Mrs. McLean, he a son of Judge McLean, of Ohio.

June 17th

On Friday evening we went to the Queen's Ball, and for the first time saw Her Majesty dance, which she does very well, and so does the Duchess of Sutherland, grandmother though she be.

On Monday evening we went to a concert given to the Queen by the Duke of Wellington at Apsley House. This was an occasion not to be forgotten, but I cannot describe it. On Tuesday I went for the first time to hear a debate upon the Portugal interference in the House of Lords. It brought out all the leaders, and I was so fortunate as to hear a most powerful speech from Lord Stanley, one from Lord Lansdowne in defence of the Ministry and one from the Duke of Wellington, who, on this occasion, sided with the Ministers. On Wednesday was the great FETE given by the Duchess of Sutherland to the Queen. It was like a chapter of a fairy tale. Persons from all the courts of Europe who were there told us that nowhere in Europe was there anything as fine as the hall and grand staircase where the Duchess received her guests. It exceeded my utmost conceptions of magnificence and beauty. The vast size of the apartment, the vaulted ceilings, the arabesque ornaments, the fine pictures, the profusion of flowers, the music, the flourish of trumpets, as the Queen passed backward and forward, the superb dresses and diamonds of the women, the parti-colored full dress of the gentlemen all contributed to make up a scene not to be forgotten. The Queen's Ball was not to be compared to it, so much more effective is Stafford House than Buckingham Palace. . . . We were fortunate to be present there, for Stafford House is not opened in this way but once in a year or two, and the Duke's health is now so very uncertain, that it may be many years before it happens again. He was not present the other evening.

LETTER: To Mr. and Mrs. I.P.D. My dear Uncle and Aunt: LONDON, June 20, 1847

On the 19th, Saturday, we breakfasted with Lady Byron and my friend, Miss Murray, at Mr. Rogers'. He and Lady Byron had not met for many, many years, and their renewal of old friendship was very interesting to witness. Mr. Rogers told me that he first introduced her to Lord Byron. After breakfast he had been repeating some lines of poetry which he thought fine, when he suddenly exclaimed: "But there is a bit of American PROSE, which, I think, had more poetry in it than almost any modern verse." He then repeated, I should think, more than a page from Dana's "Two Years Before the Mast," describing the falling overboard of one of the crew, and the effect it produced, not only at the moment, but for some time afterward. I wondered at his memory, which enabled him to recite so beautifully a long prose passage, so much more difficult than verse. Several of those present with whom the book was a favorite, were so glad to hear from me that it was as TRUE as interesting, for they had regarded it as partly a work of imagination. Lady Byron had told Mr. Rogers when she came in that Lady Lovelace, her daughter (Ada) wished also to pay him a visit, and would come after breakfast to join us for half an hour. She also had not seen Rogers, I BELIEVE, ever. Lady Lovelace joined us soon after breakfast, and as we were speaking of the enchantment of Stafford House on Wednesday evening, Mr. Rogers proposed to go over it and see its fine pictures by daylight. He immediately went himself by a short back passage through the park to ask permission and returned with all the eagerness and gallantry of a young man to say that he had obtained it. We had thus an opportunity of seeing, in the most leisurely way and in the most delightful society, the fine pictures and noble apartments of Stafford House again.

... On Tuesday Mr. Hallam took us to the British Museum, and being a director, he could enter on a private day, when we were not annoyed by a crowd, and, moreover, we had the advantage of the best interpreters and guides. We did not even enter the library, which requires a day by itself, but confined ourselves to the Antiquity rooms. . . . As I entered the room devoted to the Elgin marbles, the works of the "divine Phidias," I stepped with awe, as if entering a temple, and the Secretary, who was by my side, observing it, told me that the Grand Duke Constantine, when he came a few days before, made, as he entered, a most profound and reverential bow. This was one of my most delightful mornings, and I left the Antiquities with a stronger desire to see them again than before I had seen them at all.

Sunday, June 27th

. . . I went on Wednesday to dine at Lord Monteagle's to meet Father Mathew, and the Archbishop of Dublin (Dr. Whately) also dined there. Father Mathew spoke with great interest of America and of American liberality, and is very anxious to go to our country. He saw Mr. Forbes at Cork and spoke of him with great regard. . . . On [Saturday] Mr. Bancroft went to the palace to see the King of the Belgians, with the rest of the Diplomatic Corps. After his return we went to Westminster Hall to see the prize pictures, as Lord Lansdowne had sent us tickets for the private view. The Commission of Fine Arts have offered prizes for the best historical pictures that may serve to adorn the new Houses of Parliament, and the pictures of this collection were all painted with that view. One of those which have received a prize is John Robinson bestowing his farewell blessing upon the Pilgrims at Leyden, which is very pleasing. It was to me like a friend in a strange country, and I lingered over it the longest.

July 2d

Wednesday [evening] we went to Lady Duff Gordon's, who is the daughter of Mrs. Austin, where was a most agreeable party, and among others, Andersen, the Danish poet-author of the "Improvisatore." He has a most striking poetical physiognomy, but as he talked only German or bad French, I left him to Mr. Bancroft in the conversation way.

The next morning before nine o'clock we were told that Mr. Rogers, the poet, was downstairs. I could not imagine what had brought him out so early, but found that Moore, the poet, had come to town and would stay but a day, and we must go that very morning and breakfast with him at ten o'clock. We went and found a delightful circle. I sat between Moore and Rogers, who was in his very best humor. Moore is but a wreck, but most a interesting one.

LETTER: To Mr. and Mrs. I.P.D. Nuneham Park, July 27, 1847

My dear Uncle and Aunt: . . . I must go back to the day when my last letters were despatched, as my life since has been full of interest. On Monday evening, the 19th, we went to the French play, to see Rachel in "Phedre." She far surpassed my imagination in the expression of all the powerful passions. . . . On Tuesday Mr. Bancroft went down to hear Lord John make a speech to his constituents in the city, while I went to see Miss Burdett-Coutts lay the corner-stone of the church which "the Bishop of London has permitted her to build," to use her own expression in her note to me. In the evening we dined there with many of the clergy, and Lord Brougham, Lord Dundonald, etc. I went down with the Dean of Westminster, who was very agreeable and instructive. He and Dr. Whately have the simplicity of children, with an immense deal of knowledge, which they impart in the most pleasant way. Saturday, the 24th, we were to leave town for our first country excursion. We were invited by Dr. Hawtrey, the Head Master of Eton, to be present at the ceremonies accompanying the annual election of such boys on the Foundation as are selected to go up to King's College, Cambridge, where they are also placed on a Foundation. From reading Dr. Arnold's life you will have learned that the head master of one of these very great schools is no unimportant personage. Dr. Hawtrey has an income of six or seven thousand pounds. He is unmarried, but has two single sisters who live with him, and his establishment in one of the old college houses is full of elegance and comfort. We took an open travelling carriage with imperials, and drove down to Eton with our own horses, arriving about one o'clock. At two, precisely, the Provost of King's College, Cambridge, was to arrive, and to be received under the old gateway of the cloister by the Captain of the school with a Latin speech. After dinner there is a regatta among the boys, which is one of the characteristic and pleasing old customs. All the fashionables of London who have sons at Eton come down to witness their happiness, and the river bank is full of gayety. The evening finished with the most beautiful fireworks I ever saw, which lighted up the Castle behind and were reflected in the Thames below, while the glancing oars of the young boatmen, and the music of their band with a merry chime of bells from St. George's Chapel, above, all combined to give gayety and interest to the scene. The next morning (Sunday), after an agreeable breakfast in the long, low-walled breakfast-room, which opens upon the flower garden, we went to Windsor to worship in St. George's Chapel. The Queen's stall is rather larger than the others, and one is left vacant for the Prince of Wales.

LONDON, July 29th

And now with a new sheet I must begin my account of Nuneham. . . . The Archbishop of York is the second son of Lord Vernon, but his uncle, Earl Harcourt, dying without children, left him all his estate, upon which he took the name of Harcourt. We arrived about four o'clock. . . . The dinner was at half-past seven, and when I went down I found the Duchess of Sutherland, Lady Caroline Leveson-Gower, Lord Kildare, and several of the sons and daughters of the Archbishop. The dinner and evening passed off very agreeably. The Duchess is a most high-bred person, and thoroughly courteous. As we were going in or out of a room instead of preceding me, which was her right, she always made me take her arm, which was a delicate way of getting over her precedence. . . . At half-past nine the [next morning] we met in the drawing-room, when the Archbishop led the way down to prayers. This was a beautiful scene, for he is now ninety, and to hear him read the prayers with a firm, clear voice, while his family and dependents knelt about him was a pleasure never to be forgotten. . . . At five I was to drive round the park with the Archbishop himself in his open carriage. This drive was most charming. He explained everything, told me when such trees would be felled, and when certain tracts of underwood would be fit for cutting, how old the different-sized deer were--in short, the whole economy of an English park. Every pretty point of view, too, he made me see, and was as active and wide-awake as if he were thirty, rather than ninety. . . . The next morning, after prayers and breakfast, I took my leave.

LETTER: To A.H. BISHOP'S PALACE, NORWICH, August 1st

My dear Ann: How I wish I could transport you to the spot where I am writing, but if I could summon it before your actual vision you would take it for a dream or a romance, so different is everything within the walls which enclose the precincts of an English Cathedral from anything we can conceive on our side of the water. . . . Some of the learned people and noblemen have formed an Archaeological Society for the study and preservation [of] the interesting architectural antiquities of the kingdom, and [it] is upon the occasion of the annual meeting of this society for a week at Norwich that the Bishop has invited us to stay a few days at the palace and join them in their agreeable antiquarian excursions. We arrived on Friday at five o'clock after a long dull journey of five hours on the railway. . . . Staying in the house are our friends, Mr. and Mrs. Milman, Lord Northampton and his son, Lord Alwyne Compton, and the Bishop's family, consisting of Mrs. Stanley, and of two Miss Stanleys, agreeable and highly cultivated girls, and Mr. Arthur Stanley, the writer of Dr. Arnold's Biography.

After dinner company soon arrived. Among them were Mrs. Opie, who resides here. She is a pleasing, lively old lady, in full Quaker dress. The most curious feature of the evening was a visit which the company paid to the cellar and kitchen, which were lighted up for the occasion. They were build by the old Norman bishops of the twelfth century, and had vaulted stone roofs as beautifully carved and ribbed as a church.

The next day, Saturday, the antiquarians made a long excursion to hunt up some ruins, while the Milmans, Mr. Stanley, and ourselves, went to visit the place of Lady Suffield, about twelve miles distant, and which is the most perfect specimen of the Elizabethan style. Lady Suffield herself is as Elizabethan as her establishment;

she is of one [of] the oldest high Tory families and so opposed to innovations of all sorts that though her letters, which used to arrive at two, before the opening of the railway two years ago, now arrive at seven in the morning, they are never allowed to be brought till the old hour. . . . This morning Mr. Bancroft and the rest are gone on an excursion to Yarmouth to see some ruins, while I remain here to witness the chairing of two new members of Parliament, who have just been elected, of whom Lord Douro, son of the Duke of Wellington, is one.

LETTER: To I.P.D. AUDLEY END, October 14, 1847

Dear Uncle: We are staying for a few days at Lord Braybrooke's place, one of the most magnificent in England; but before I say a word about it I must tell you of A.'s safe arrival and how happy I have been made by having him with me again. . . . On Saturday the 9th we had the honor of dining with the LORD MAYOR to meet the Duke of Cambridge, a FETE so unlike anything else and accompanied by so many old and peculiar customs that I must describe it to you at full length. The Mansion House is in the heart of the CITY, and is very magnificent and spacious, the Egyptian Hall, as the dining-room is called, being one of the noblest apartments I have seen. The guests were about 250 in number and were received by the Lady Mayoress SITTING. When dinner was announced, the Lord Mayor went out first, preceded by the sword-bearer and mace-bearer and all the insignia of office. Then came the Duke of Cambridge and the Lady Mayoress, then Mr. Bancroft and I together, which is the custom at these great civic feasts. We marched through the long gallery by the music of the band to the Egyptian Hall, where two raised seats like thrones were provided for the Lord Mayor and Mayoress at the head of the hall. On the right hand of the Lord Mayor sat the Duke of Cambridge in a COMMON CHAIR, for royalty yields entirely to the Mayor, on his own ground. On the right of the Duke of Cambridge sat the Mayoress- elect (for the present dignitaries go out of office on the 1st of November). On the left hand of the present Lady Mayoress sat the Lord Mayor-ELECT, then I came with my husband on my left hand in very conjugal style.

There were three tables the whole length of the hall, and that at which we were placed went across at the head. When we are placed, the herald stands behind the Lord Mayor and cries: "My Lords, Ladies, and Gentlemen, pray silence, for grace." Then the chaplain in his gown, goes behind the Lord Mayor and says grace. After the second course two large gold cups, nearly two feet high, are placed before the Mayor and Mayoress. The herald then cries with a loud voice: "His Royal Highness the Duke of Cambridge, the American Minister, the Lord Chief Baron," etc., etc. (enumerating about a dozen of the most distinguished guests), "and ladies and gentlemen all, the Lord Mayor and Lady Mayoress do bid you most heartily welcome and invite you to drink in a loving cup." Whereupon the Mayor and Mayoress rise and each turn to their next neighbor, who take off the cover while they drink. After my right-hand neighbor, the Lord Mayor-elect, had put on the cover, he turns to me and says, "Please take off the cover," which I do and hold it while he drinks; then I replace the cover and turn round to Mr. Bancroft, who rises and performs the same office for me while I drink; then he turns to his next neighbor, who takes off the cover for him. I have not felt so solemn since I stood up to be married as when Mr. Bancroft and I were standing up alone together, the rest of the company looking on, I with this great heavy gold cup in my hand, so heavy that I could scarcely lift it to my mouth with both hands, and he with the cover before me, with rather a mischievous expression in his face. Then came two immense gold platters filled with rose water, which were also passed round. These gold vessels were only used by the persons at the head table; the other guests were served with silver cups. When the dessert and the wine are placed on the table, the herald says, "My Lords, Ladies, and Gentlemen, please to charge your glasses." After we duly charge our glasses the herald cries: "Lords, Ladies, and Gentlemen, pray silence for the Lord Mayor." He then rises and proposes the first toast, which is, of course, always "The Queen." After a time came the "American Minister," who was obliged to rise up at my elbow and respond. We got home just after twelve.

And now let me try to give you some faint idea of Audley End, which is by far the most magnificent house I have seen yet. It was built by the Earl of Suffolk, son of the Duke of Norfolk who was beheaded in Elizabeth's reign for high treason, upon the site of an abbey, the lands of which had been granted by the crown to that powerful family. One of the Earls of Suffolk dying without sons, the EARLDOM passed into another branch and the BARONY and ESTATE of Howard de Walden came into the female line. In course of time, a Lord Howard de Walden dying without a son, his title also passed into another family, but his estate went to his nephew, Lord Braybrooke, the father of the present Lord. Lady Braybrooke is the daughter of the Marquis of Cornwallis, and granddaughter of our American Lord Cornwallis.

The house is of the Elizabethan period and is one of the best preserved specimens of that style, but of its vast extent and magnificence I can give you no idea. We arrived about five o'clock, and were ushered through an immense hall of carved oak hung with banners up a fine staircase to the grand saloon, where we were received by the host and hostess. Now of this grand saloon I must try to give you a conception. It was, I should think, from seventy- five to one hundred feet in length. The ceiling overhead was very rich with hanging corbels, like stalactites, and the entire walls were panelled, with a full-length family portrait in each panel, which was arched at the top, so that the whole wall was composed of these round-topped pictures with rich gilding between. Notwithstanding its vast size, the sofas and tables were so disposed all over the apartment as to give it the most friendly, warm, and social aspect.

Lady Braybrooke herself ushered me to my apartments, which were the state rooms. First came Mr. Bancroft's dressing-room, where was a blazing fire. Then came the bedroom, with the state bed of blue and gold, covered with embroidery, and with the arms and coronet of Howard de Walden. The walls were hung with crimson and white damask, and the sofas and chairs also, and it was surrounded by pictures, among others a full length of Queen Charlotte, just opposite the foot of the bed, always saluted me every morning when I awoke, with her fan, her hoop, and her deep ruffles.

My dressing-room, which was on the opposite side from Mr. Bancroft's, was a perfect gem. It was painted by the famous Rebecco who came over from Italy to ornament so many of the great English houses at one time. The whole ceiling and walls were covered with beautiful designs and with gilding, and a beautiful recess for a couch was supported by fluted gilded columns; the architraves and mouldings of the doors were gilt, and the panels of the doors were filled with Rebecco's beautiful designs. The chairs were of light blue embroidered with thick, heavy gold, and all this bearing the stamp of antiquity was a thousand times more interesting than mere modern splendor. In the centre of the room was a toilet of white muslin (universal here), and on it a gilt dressing-glass, which gave pretty effect to the whole.

I sat at dinner between Lord Braybrooke and Sir John Boileau, and found them both very agreeable. The dining-room is as magnificent as the other apartments. The ceiling is in the Elizabethan style, covered with figures, and the walls white and gold panelling hung with full-length family portraits not set into the wall like the saloon, but in frames. In the evening the young people had a round game at cards and the elder ones seemed to prefer talking to a game at whist. The ladies brought down their embroidery or netting. At eleven a tray with wine and water is brought in and a quantity of bed candlesticks, and everybody retires when they like. The next morning the guests assembled at half-past nine in the great gallery which leads to the chapel to go in together to prayers. The chapel is really a beautiful little piece of architecture, with a vaulted roof and windows of painted glass. On one side is the original cast of the large monument to Lord Cornwallis (our lord) which is in Westminster Abbey. After breakfast we passed a couple of hours in going all over the house, which is in perfect keeping in every part.

We returned to the library, a room as splendid as the saloon, only instead of pictured panels it was surrounded by books in beautiful gilt bindings. In the immense bay window was a large Louis Quatorze table, round which the ladies all placed themselves at their embroidery, though I preferred looking over curious illuminated missals, etc., etc.

The next day was the meeting of the County Agricultural Society. . . . At the hour appointed we all repaired to the ground where the prizes were to be given out. . . . Lord Braybrooke made first a most paternal and interesting address, which showed me in the most favorable view the relation between the noble and the lower class in England, a relation which must depend much on the personal character of the lord of the manor. . . . First came prizes to ploughmen, then the plough boys, then the shepherds, then to such peasants as had reared many children without aid, then to women who had been many years in the same farmer's service, etc., etc. A clock was awarded to a poor man and his wife who had reared six children and buried seven without aid from the parish. The rapture with which Mr. and Mrs. Flitton and the whole six children gazed on this clock, an immense treasure for a peasant's cottage, was both comic and affecting. . . . The next morning we made our adieus to our kind host and hostess, and set off for London, accompanied by Sir John Tyrrell, Major Beresford, and young Mr. Boileau.

LETTER: To W.D.B. LONDON,
November 4, 1847

Dear W.: . . . Mr. Bancroft and I dined on Friday, the 22d, with Mr. and Mrs. Hawes, under-Secretary of State, to meet Mr. Brooke, the Rajah of Sarawak, who is a great lion in London just now. He is an English gentleman of large fortune who has done much to Christianize Borneo, and to open its trade to the English. I sat between him and Mr. Ward, formerly Minister to Mexico before Mr. Pakenham. He wrote a very nice book on Mexico, and is an agreeable and intelligent person. . . . On Wednesday A. and I went together to the National Gallery, and just as we were setting out Mr. Butler of New York came in and I invited him to join us. . . . While we were seated before a charming Claude who should come in but Mr. R.W. Emerson and we had quite a joyful greeting. Just then came in Mr. Rogers with two ladies, one on each arm. He renewed his request that I would bring my son to breakfast with him, and appointed Friday morning, and then added if those gentlemen who are with you are your friends and countrymen, perhaps they will accompany you. They very gladly acceded, and I was thankful Mr. Emerson had chanced to be with me at that moment as it procured him a high pleasure.

Yesterday your father and I dined with Sir George Grey. . . . About four o'clock came on such a fog as I have not seen in London, and the newspapers of this morning speak of it as greater than has been known for many years. Sir George Grey lives in Eaton Place, which is parallel and just behind Eaton Square. In going that little distance, though there is a brilliant gas light at every door, the coachman was completely bewildered, and lost himself entirely. We could only walk the horses, the footman exploring ahead. When the guests by degrees arrived, there was the same rejoicing as if we had met on Mont St. Bernard after a contest with an Alpine snow-storm. . . . Lady Grey told me she was dining with the Queen once in one of these tremendous fogs, and that many of the guests did not arrive till dinner was half through, which was horrible at a royal dinner; but the elements care little for royalty.

November 14th

On Saturday we dined at the Duc de Broglie's. He married the daughter of Madam de Stael, but she is not now living. I was very agreeably placed with Mr. Macaulay on one side of me, so that I found it more pleasant than diplomatic dinners usually. At the English tables we meet people who know each other well, and have a common culture and tastes and habits of familiarity, and a fund of pleasant stories, but of course, at foreign tables, they neither know each other or the English so well as to give the same easy flow to conversation. I am afraid we are the greatest diners-out in London, but we are brought into contact a great deal with the literary and Parliamentary people, which our colleagues know little about, as also with the clergy and the judges. I should not be willing to make it the habit of my life, but it is time not misspent during the years of our abode here. . . . The good old Archbishop of York is dead, and I am glad I paid my visit to him when I did. Mr. Rogers has paid me a long visit to-day and gave me all the particulars of his death. It was a subject I should not have introduced, for of that knot of intimate friends, Mr. Grenville, the Archbishop, and himself, he is now all that remains.

November 28th

. . . On Monday evening I went without Mr. Bancroft to a little party at Mrs. Lyell's, where I was introduced to Mrs. Somerville. She has resided for the last nine years abroad, chiefly at Venice, but has now come to London and taken a house very near us. . . . Her daughter told me that nothing could exceed the ease and simplicity with which her literary occupations were carried on. She is just publishing a book upon Natural Geography without regard to political boundaries. She writes principally before she rises in the morning on a little piece of board, with her inkstand on a table by her side. After she leaves her room she is as much at leisure as other people, but if an idea strikes her she takes her little board into a corner or window and writes quietly for a short time and returns to join the circle.

Dr. Somerville told me that his wife did not discover her genius for mathematics till she was about sixteen. Her brother, who has no talent for it, was receiving a mathematical lesson from a master while she was hemming and stitching in the room. In this way she first heard the problems of Euclid stated and was ravished. When the lesson was over, she carried off the book to her room and devoured it. For a long time she pursued her studies secretly, as she had scaled heights of science which were not considered feminine by those about her.

December 2d

I put down my pen yesterday when the carriage came to the door for my drive. It was a day bright, beaming, and exhilarating as one of our own winter days. I was so busy enjoying the unusual beams of the unclouded sun that I did not perceive for some time that I had left my muff, and was obliged to drive home again to get it. While I was waiting in the carriage for the footman to get it, two of the most agreeable old-lady faces in the world presented themselves at the window. They were the Miss Berrys. They had driven up behind me and got out to have a little talk on the sidewalk. I took them into Mr. Bancroft's room and was thankful that my muff had sent me back to receive a visit which at their age is rarely paid. . . . I found them full of delight at Mr. Brooke, the Rajah of Sarawak, with whose nobleness of soul they would have great sympathy. He is just now the lion of London, and like all other lions is run after by most people because he is one, and by the few because he deserves to be one. Now, lest you should know nothing about him, let me tell you that at his own expense he fitted out a vessel, and established himself at Borneo, where he soon acquired so great [an] ascendancy over the native Rajah, that he insisted on resigning to him the government of his province of Sarawak. Here, with only three European companions, by moral and intellectual force alone, he succeeded in suppressing piracy and civil war among the natives and opened a trade with the interior of Borneo which promises great advantages to England. . . . Everybody here has the INFLUENZA--a right-down influenza, that sends people to their beds. Those who have triumphed at their exemption in the evening, wake up perhaps in the morning full of aches in every limb, and scoff no longer. . . . Dinner parties are sometimes quite broken up by the excuses that come pouring in at the last moment. Lady John Russell had seven last week at a small dinner of twelve; 1,200 policemen at one time were taken off duty, so that the thieves might have had their own way, but they were probably as badly off themselves.

LETTER: To Mr. and Mrs. I.P.D. LONDON, December 16, 1847

My dear Uncle and Aunt: . . . On Saturday Mr. Hallam wrote us that Sir Robert Peel had promised to breakfast with him on Monday morning and he thought we should like to meet him in that quiet way. So we presented ourselves at ten o'clock, and were joined by Sir Robert, Lord Mahon, Macaulay, and Milman, who with Hallam himself, formed a circle that could not be exceeded in the wide world. I was the only lady, except Miss Hallam; but I am especially favored in the breakfast line. I would cross the Atlantic only for the pleasure I had that morning in hearing such men talk for two or three hours in an entirely easy unceremonious breakfast way. Sir Robert was full of stories, and showed himself as much the scholar as the statesman. Macaulay was overflowing as usual, and Lord Mahon and Milman are full of learning and accomplishments. The classical scholarship of these men is very perfect and sometimes one catches a glimpse of awfully deep abysses of learning. But then it is ONLY a glimpse, for their learning has no cumbrous and dull pedantry about it. They are all men of society and men of the world, who keep up with it everywhere. There is many a pleasant story and many a good joke, and everything discussed but politics, which, as Sir Robert and Macaulay belong to opposite dynasties, might be dangerous ground.

After dinner we went a little before ten to Lady Charlotte Lindsay's. She came last week to say that she was to have a little dinner on Monday and wished us to come in afterwards. This is universal here, and is the easiest and most agreeable form of society. She had Lord Brougham and Colonel and Mrs. Dawson-Damer, etc., to dine. . . . Mrs. Damer wished us to come the next evening to her in the same way, just to get our cup of tea. These nice little teas are what you need in Boston. There is no supper, no expense, nothing but society. Mrs. Damer is the grand-daughter of the beautiful Lady Waldegrave, the niece of Horace Walpole, who married the Duke of Gloucester. She was left an orphan at a year old and was confided by her mother to the care of Mrs. Fitzherbert. She lived with her until her marriage and was a great pet of George IV, and tells a great many interesting stories of him and Mrs. Fitzherbert, who was five years older than he.

LETTER: To W.D.B. LONDON,
December 30, 1847

Dear W.: Your father left me on the 18th to go to Paris. This is the best of all seasons for him to be there, for the Ministers are all out of town at Christmas, and in Paris everything is at its height. My friends are very kind to me--those who remain in town. . . . One day I dined at Sir Francis Simpkinson's and found a pleasant party. Lady Simpkinson is a sister of Lady Franklin, whom I was very glad to meet, as she has been in America and knows many Americans, Mrs. Kirkland for one. . . . Then I have passed one evening for the first time at Mr. Tagent's, the Unitarian clergyman, where I met many of the literary people who are out of the great world, and yet very desirable to see.

There, too, I met the Misses Cushman, Charlotte and Susan, who attend his church. I was very much pleased with both of them. I have never seen them play, but they will send me a list of their parts at their next engagement and I shall certainly go to hear them. They are of Old Colony descent (from Elder Cushman), and have very much of the New England character, culture, and good sense. On Monday I dined at Sir Edward Codrington's, the hero of Navarino, with the Marquis and Marchioness of Queensberry, and a party of admirals and navy officers. On Tuesday I dined at Lady Braye's, where were Mr. Rogers, Dr. Holland, Sir Augustus and Lady Albinia Foster, formerly British Minister to the United States. He could describe OUR COURT, as he called it, in the time of Madison and Monroe.

January 1, 1848

This evening, in addition to my usual morning letter from your father, I have another; a new postal arrangement beginning to-day with the New Year. He gives me a most interesting conversation he has just been having with Baron von Humboldt, who is now in Paris. He says he poured out a delicious stream of remarks, anecdotes, narratives, opinion. He feels great interest in our Mexican affairs, as he has been much there, and is a Mexican by adoption.

His letter, dated the 31st December, says: "Madam Adelaide died at three this morning." This death astonished me, for he saw her only a few evenings since at the Palace. She was a woman of strong intellect and character, and her brother, the King, was very much attached to her as a counsellor and friend. . . . There were more than 100 Americans to be presented on New Year's Day at Paris, and, as Madam Adelaide's death took place without a day's warning, you can imagine the embroidered coats and finery which were laid on the shelf.

Saturday, January 7th

Yesterday, my dear son, I had a delightful dinner at the dear Miss Berrys. They drove to the door on Thursday and left a little note to say, "Can you forgive a poor sick soul for not coming to you before, when you were all alone," and begging me to come the next day at seven, to dine. There was Lady Charlotte and Lady Stuart de Rothesay, who was many years ambassadress at Paris, and very agreeable. Then there was Dr. Holland and Mr. Stanley, the under- Secretary of State, etc. In the evening came quite an additional party, and I passed it most pleasantly. . . . Your father writes that on Friday he dined at Thiers' with Mignet, Cousin, Pontois, and Lord Normanby. He says such a dinner is "unique in a man's life." "Mignet is delightful, frank, open, gay, full of intelligence, and of that grace which makes society charming." . . . Your father to- day gives me some account of Thiers. He is now fifty: he rises at five o'clock every morning, toils till twelve, breakfasts, makes researches, and then goes to the Chambers. In the evening he always receives his friends except Wednesdays and Thursdays, when he attends his wife to the opera and to the Academie.

LETTER: To Mr. and Mrs. I.P.D. LONDON, January 28th, 1848

My dear Uncle and Aunt: . . . Last Monday I received [this] note from George Sumner, which I thought might interest you: "My dear Mrs. Bancroft: I hasten to congratulate you upon an event most honorable to Mr. Bancroft and to our country. The highest honor which can be bestowed in France upon a foreigner has just been conferred on him. He was chosen this afternoon a Corresponding Member of the Institute. Five names were presented for the vacant chair of History. Every vote but one was in favor of Mr. Bancroft (that one for Mr. Grote of London, author of the 'History of Greece'). A gratifying fact in regard to this election is that it comes without the knowledge of Mr. Bancroft, and without any of those preliminary visits on his part, and those appeals to academicians whose votes are desired, that are so common with candidates for vacancies at the Institute. The honor acquires double value for being unsought, and I have heard with no small satisfaction several Members of the Academy contrast the modest reserve of Mr. Bancroft with the restless manoeuvres to which they have been accustomed. Prescott, you know, is already a member, and I think America may be satisfied with two out of seven of a class of History which is selected from the world."

LETTER: To T.D. LONDON, February 24, 1848

My dear Brother: . . . Great excitement exists in London to-day at the reception of the news from France. Guizot is overthrown, and Count Mole is made Prime Minister. The National Guards have sided with the people, and would not fire upon them, and that secret of the weakness of the army being revealed, I do not see why the Liberal party cannot obtain all they want in the end. Louis Philippe has sacrificed the happiness of France for the advancement of his own family, but nations in the nineteenth [century] have learned that they were not made to be the slaves of a dynasty. Mr. Bancroft dines with the French Minister to-day, not with a party, but quite EN FAMILLE, and he will learn there what the hopes and fears of the Government are.

February 25th

The news this morning is only from Amiens, which has risen in support of France. The railways are torn up all round Paris, to prevent the passage of troops, and the roads and barriers are all in possession of the people. All France will follow the lead of Paris, and what will be the result Heaven only knows.

LETTER: To I.P.D. LONDON, February 26, 1848

My dear Uncle: . . . On Thursday Mr. Bancroft dined with Count Jarnac, the Minister in the Duc de Broglie's absence, and he little dreamed of the blow awaiting him. The fortifications and the army seemed to make the King quite secure. On Friday Mr. Bancroft went to dine with Kenyon, and I drove there with him for a little air. On my return Cates, the butler, saluted me with the wondrous news of the deposition and flight of the royal family, which Mr. Brodhead had rushed up from his club to impart to us. I was engaged to a little party at Mr. Hallam's, where I found everybody in great excitement.

Sunday Noon

To-day we were to have dined with Baron de Rothschild, but this morning I got a note from the beautiful baroness, saying that her sister-in-law and her mother with three children, had just arrived from Paris at her house in the greatest distress, without a change of clothes, and in deep anxiety about the Baron, who had stayed behind.

Our colleagues all look bewildered and perplexed beyond measure. . . . The English aristocracy have no love for Louis Philippe, but much less for a republic, so near at hand, and everybody seemed perplexed and uneasy.

Tuesday

On Sunday the Duc de Nemours arrived at the French Embassy, and Monday the poor Duchess de Montpensier, the innocent cause of all the trouble. No one knows where the Duchess de Nemours and her young children are, and the King and Queen are entirely missing. At one moment it is reported that he is drowned, and then, again, at Brussels.

Wednesday

To-day the French Embassy have received despatches announcing the new government, and Count Jarnac has immediately resigned. This made it impossible for the Duc de Nemours and the Duchess de Montpensier to remain at the Embassy, and they fell by inheritance to Mr. Van de Weyer, whose Queen is Louis Philippe's daughter. The Queen has taken Louis Philippe's daughter, Princess Clementine, who married Prince Auguste de Saxe-Coburg to the Palace, but for State Policy's sake she can do nothing about the others. Mr. Van de Weyer offered Mr. Bates's place of East Sheen, which was most gratefully accepted.

Friday

This morning came Thackeray, who is the soul of PUNCH, and showed me a piece he had written for the next number.

Saturday

The King has arrived. What a crossing of the Channel, pea-jacket, woollen comforter, and all! The flight is a perfect comedy, and if PUNCH had tried to invent anything more ludicrous, it would have failed. Panic, despotism, and cowardice.

These things are much more exciting here than across the water. We are so near the scene of action and everybody has a more personal interest here in all these matters. The whole week has been like a long play, and now, on Saturday night, I want nothing but repose. What a dream it must be to the chief actors! The Queen, who is always good and noble, was averse to such ignominious flight; she preferred staying and taking what came, and if Madam Adelaide had lived, they would never have made such a [word undecipherable] figure. Her pride and courage would have inspired them. With her seemed to fly Louis Philippe's star, as Napoleon's with Josephine. . . . Mr. Emerson has just come to London and we give him a dinner on Tuesday, the 14th. Several persons wish much to see him, and Monckton Milnes reviewed him in BLACKWOOD.

LETTER: To W.D.B. LONDON, March 11, 1848

Dear W.: . . . Yesterday we dined at Lord Lansdowne's. Among the guests were M. and Madam Van de Weyer, and Mrs. Austin, the translatress, who has been driven over here from Paris, where she has resided for several years. She is a vehement friend of Guizot's, though a bitter accuser of Louis Philippe, but how can they be separated? She interests herself strongly now in all his arrangements, and is assisting his daughters to form their humble establishment. He and his daughters together have about eight hundred pounds a year, and that in London is poverty. They have taken a small house in Brompton Square, a little out of town, and one of those suburban, unfashionable regions where the most accommodations can be had at the least price. What a change for those who have witnessed their almost regal receptions in Paris! The young ladies bear very sweetly all their reverses. . . . Guizot, himself, I hear, is as FIER as ever, and almost gay. Princess de Lieven is here at the "Clarendon," and their friendship is as great as ever.

March 15th

Yesterday we had an agreeable dinner at our own house. Macaulay, Milman, Lord Morpeth and Monckton Milnes were all most charming, and we ladies listened with eager ears. Conversation was never more interesting than just now, in this great crisis of the world's affairs. Mr. Emerson was here and seemed to enjoy [it] much.

Friday, March 17th

Things look rather darker in France, but we ought not to expect a republic to be established without some difficulties. . . . You cannot judge of the state of France, however, through the medium of the English newspapers, for, of course, English sympathies are all entirely against it. They never like France, and a republic of any kind still less. A peaceful and prosperous republic in the heart of Europe would be more deprecated than a state of anarchy. The discussion of French matters reveals to me every moment the deep repugnance of the English to republican institutions. It lets in a world of light upon opinions and feelings, which, otherwise, would not have been discovered by me.

Sunday, March 19th

Yesterday we breakfasted at Mrs. Milman's. I was the only lady, but there were Macaulay, Hallam, Lord Morpeth, and, above all, Charles Austin, whom I had not seen before, as he never dines out, but who is the most striking talker in England. He has made a fortune by the law in the last few years, which gives him an income of 8,000 pounds. He has the great railroad cases which come before the House of Lords. . . . On Tuesday came a flying report of a revolution in Berlin, but no one believed it. We concluded it rather a speculation of the newsmen, who are hawking revolutions after every mail in second and third editions. We were going that evening to a SOIREE at Bunsen's, whom we found cheerful as ever and fearing no evil. On Monday the news of the revolution in Austria produced a greater sensation even than France, for it was the very pivot of conservatism. . . . On Thursday I received the letter from A. at eight A.M., which I enclose to you. It gives an account of the revolution in Berlin.

LETTER: To T.D. March 31

The old world is undergoing a complete reorganization, and is unfolding a rapid series of events more astonishing than anything in history. Where it will stop, and what will be its results, nobody can tell. Royalty has certainly not added to its respectability by its conduct in its time of trial. Since the last steamer went, Italy has shaken off the Austrian yoke, Denmark has lost her German provinces, Poland has risen, or is about to rise, which will bring Russia thundering down upon Liberal Europe. . . . Our whole Diplomatic Corps are certainly "in a fix," and we are really the only members of it who have any reason to be quite at ease. Two or three have been called home to be Ministers of Foreign Affairs, as they have learned something of constitutional liberty in England. England is, as yet, all quiet, and I hope will keep so, but the Chartists are at work and Ireland is full of inflammable matter. But England does love her institutions, and is justly proud of their comparative freedom, and long may she enjoy them. . . . On Sunday Mr. Emerson dined with us with Lady Morgan and Mrs. Jameson--the authoress. On Monday I took him to a little party at Lady Morgan's. His works are a good deal known here. I have great pleasure in seeing so old a friend so far from home. . . . I think we shall have very few of our countrymen out this spring, as travelling Europe is so uncertain, with everything in commotion. Those who are passing the winter in Italy are quite shut in at present, and if war begins, no one knows where it will spread.

LETTER: To W.D.B. LONDON, April 7, 1848

. . . On Wednesday we had an agreeable dinner at Mrs. Milner Gibson's. Mr. and Mrs. Disraeli, Mr. and Mrs. Sheridan (brother of Mrs. Norton), etc., were among the guests. After dinner I had a very long talk with Disraeli. He is, you know, of the ultra Tory party here, and looks at the Continental movements from the darkest point of view. He cannot admit as a possibility the renovation of European society upon more liberal principles, and considers it as the complete dissolution of European civilization which will, like Asia, soon present but the ashes of a burnt-out flame. This is most atheistic, godless, and un-christian doctrine, and he cannot himself believe it. The art of printing and the rapid dissemination of thought changes all these things in our days.

LETTER: To I.P.D. April 10

This is the day of the "Great Chartist Meeting," which has terrified all London to the last degree, I think most needlessly. The city and town is at this moment stiller than I have ever known it, for not a carriage dares to be out. Nothing is to be seen but a "special constable" (every gentleman in London is sworn into that office), occasionally some on foot, some on horseback, scouring the streets. I took a drive early this morning with Mr. Bancroft, and nothing could be less like the eve of a revolution. This evening, when the petition is to be presented, may bring some disturbance, not from the Chartists themselves, but from the disorderly persons who may avail themselves of the occasion. The Queen left town on Saturday for the Isle of Wight, as she had so lately been confined it was feared her health might suffer from any agitation. . . . I passed a long train of artillery on Saturday evening coming into town, which was the most earnest looking thing I have seen. . . . To-day we were to have dined at Mrs. Mansfield's, but her dinner was postponed from the great alarm about the Chartists. There is not the slightest danger of a revolution in England. The upper middle- class, which on the continent is entirely with the people, the professional and mercantile class, is here entirely conservative, and without that class no great changes can ever be made. The Duc de Montebello said of France, that he "knew there were lava streams below, but he did not know the crust was so thin." Here, on the contrary, the crust is very thick. And yet I can see in the most conservative circles that a feeling is gaining ground that some concessions must be made. An enlargement of the suffrage one hears now often discussed as, perhaps, an approaching necessity.

Friday, April 14

The day of the Chartists passed off with most ridiculous quiet, and the government is stronger than ever. . . . If the Alien Bill passes, our American friends must mind their p's and q's, for if they praise the "model republic" too loudly, they may be packed off at any time, particularly if they have "long beards," for it seems to be an axiom here that beards, mustaches, and barricades are cousins-german at least. . . . Mr. Bancroft goes to Paris on Monday, the 17th, to pass the Easter holidays. He will go on with his manuscripts, and at the same time witness the elections and meeting of the Convention.

LETTER: To W.D.B. LONDON, April 19, 1848

Dear W.: ... To-day I have driven down to Richmond to lunch with Mrs. Drummond, who is passing Easter holidays there. On coming home I found a letter from Mr. Bancroft from which I will make some extracts, as he has the best sources of knowledge in Paris. "Then I went to Mignet, who, you know, is politically the friend of Thiers. He pointed out to me the condition of France, and drew for me a picture of what it was and of the change. I begin to see the difference between France and us. Here they are accustomed to BE governed. WE are accustomed to GOVERN. HERE power may be seized and exercised, if exercised in a satisfactory manner; with us the foundation of power, its constitutionality and the legality of its acts are canvassed and analyzed. Here an unpopularity is made away with by a revolution, and you know how WE deal with it. Thus, power, if in favor, may dare anything, and if out of favor is little likely to be forgiven." ... "Our fathers had to unite the thirteen States; here they have unity enough and run no risk but from the excess of it. My hopes are not less than they were, but all that France needs may not come at once. We were fourteen years in changing our confederation into a union, perhaps France cannot be expected to jump at once into perfect legislation or perfect forms. Crude ideas are afloat, but as to Communism, it is already exploded, or will be brushed away from legislative power as soon as the National Assembly meets, though the question of ameliorating the condition of the laboring class is more and more engaging the public mind." ... "I spent an hour with Cousin, the Minister of a morning. He gave me sketches of many of the leading men of these times, and I made him detail to me he scene of Louis Philippe's abdication, which took place in a manner quite different from what I had heard in London." ... "Cousin, by the way, says that the Duc de Nemours throughout, behaved exceedingly well. Thence to the Club de la Nouvelle Republique. Did not think much of the speaking which I heard. From the club I went to Thiers, where I found Cousin and Mignet and one or two more. Some change since I met him. A leader of opposition, then a prime minister, and now left aground by the shifting tide." . . . "Everybody has given up Louis Philippe, everybody considers the nonsense of Louis Blanc as drawing to its close. The delegates from Paris will full half be UNIVERSALLY acceptable. Three-fourths of the provincial delegates will be MODERATE republicans. The people are not in a passion. They go quietly enough about their business of constructing new institutions. Ledru-Rollin, Louis Blanc, and Flocon tried to lead the way to ill, but Lamartine, whose heroism passes belief and activity passes human power, won the victory over them, found himself on Sunday, and again yesterday, sustained by all Paris, and has not only conquered but CONCILIATED them, and everybody is now firmly of opinion that the Republic will be established quietly." . . . "But while there are no difficulties from the disorderly but what can easily be overcome, the want of republican and political experience, combined with vanity and self-reliance and idealism, may throw impediments in the way of what the wisest wish, VIZ., two elected chambers and a president."

LETTER: To W.D.B. LONDON, May 5, 1848

My dear W.: ... Last evening, Thursday, we went to see Jenny Lind, on her first appearance this year. She was received with enthusiasm, and the Queen still more so. It was the first time the Queen had been at the opera since the birth of her child, and since the republican spirit was abroad, and loyalty burst out in full force. Now loyalty is very novel, and pleasant to witness, to us who have never known it.

LONDON, May 31, 1848

... Now for my journal, which has gone lamely on since the 24th of February. The Queen's Ball was to take place the evening on which I closed my last letter. My dress was a white crepe over white satin, with flounces of Honiton lace looped up with pink tuberoses. A wreath of tuberoses and bouquet for the corsage. We had tickets sent us to go through the garden and set down at a private door, which saves waiting in the long line of carriages for your turn. The Diplomatic Corps arrange themselves in a line near the door at which the Queen enters the suite of rooms, which was at ten precisely. She passes through, curtseying and bowing very gracefully, until she reaches the throne in the next room, where she and the Duchess of Cambridge, the Duchess of Saxe-Weimar and her daughters, who are here on a visit, etc., sit down, while Prince Albert, the Prince of Prussia and other sprigs of royalty stand near. The dancing soon began in front of the canopy, but the Queen herself did not dance on account of her mourning for Prince Albert's grandmother. There was another band and dancing in other rooms at the same time. After seeing several dances here the Queen and her suite move by the flourish of trumpets to another room, the guests forming a lane as she passes, bowing and smiling. Afterward she made a similar progress to supper, her household officers moving backwards before her, and her ladies and royal relatives and friends following. At half-past one Her Majesty retired and the guests departed, such as did not have to wait two hours for their carriages. On Saturday we went at two to the FETE of flowers at Chiswick, and at half-past seven dined at Lord Monteagle's to meet Monsieur and Mademoiselle Guizot. He has the finest head in the world, but his person is short and insignificant.

On Wednesday we dined at Lady Chantrey's to meet a charming party. Afterward we went to a magnificent ball at the Duke of Devonshire's, with all the great world. On Friday we went to Faraday's lecture at the Royal Institution. We went in with the Duke and Duchess of Northumberland, and I sat by her during the lecture. On Saturday was the Queen's Birthday Drawing-Room. . . . Mr. Bancroft dined at Lord Palmerston's with all the diplomats, and I went in the evening with a small party of ladies. On coming home we drove round to see the brilliant birthday illuminations. The first piece of intelligence I heard at Lady Palmerston's was the death of the Princess Sophia, an event which is a happy release for her, for she was blind and a great sufferer. It has overturned all court festivities, of course, for the present, and puts us all in deep mourning, which is not very convenient just now, in the brilliant season, and when we had all our dress arrangements made. The Queen was to have a concert to-night, a drawing-room next Friday, and a ball on the 16th, which are all deferred. . . . I forgot to say that I got a note from Miss Coutts on Sunday, asking me to go with her the next day to see the Chinese junk, so at three the next day we repaired to her house. Her sisters (Miss Burdetts) and Mr. Rogers were all the party. At the junk for the first time I saw Metternich and the Princess, his wife.

LETTER: To W.D.B. LONDON, June 29, 1848

My dear W.: . . . When I last left off I was going to dine at Miss Coutts's to meet the Duchess of Cambridge. The party was brilliant, including the Duke of Wellington, Lord and Lady Douro, Lady Jersey and the beautiful Lady Clementina Villiers, her daughter, etc. When royal people arrive everybody rises and remains standing while they stand, and if they approach you or look at you, you must perform the lowest of "curtsies." The courtesy made to royalty is very like the one I was taught to make when a little girl at Miss Tuft's school in Plymouth. One sinks down instead of stepping back in dancing-school fashion. After dinner the Duchess was pleased to stand until the gentlemen rejoined us; of course, we must all stand. . . . The next day we dined at the Lord Mayor's to meet the Ministers. This was a most interesting affair. We had all the peculiar ceremonies which I described to you last autumn, but in addition the party was most distinguished, and we had speeches from Lord Lansdowne, Lord Palmerston, Lord John, Lord Auckland, Sir George Grey, etc.

LETTER: To W.D.B. LONDON, July 21, 1848

I was truly grieved that the last steamer should go to Boston without a line from me, but I was in Yorkshire and you must forgive me. . . . I left off with the 26th of June. . . . The next evening was the Queen's Concert, which was most charming. I sat very near the Duke of Wellington, who often spoke to me between the songs. . . . The next day we went with Miss Coutts to her bank, lunched there, and went all over the building. Then we went to the Tower and the Tunnel together, she never having seen either. So ignorant are the West End people of city lions. . . . And now comes my pleasant Yorkshire excursion. We left London, at half-past three, at distance of 180 miles. This was Saturday, July 8. At York we found Mr. Hudson ready to receive us and conduct us to a special train which took us eighteen miles on the way to Newby Park, and there we found carriages to take us four miles to our destination. We met at dinner and found our party to consist of the Duke of Richmond, Lord Lonsdale, Lord George Bentinck, Lord Ingestre, Lord John Beresford, Lady Webster, whose husband, now dead, was the son of Lady Holland, two or three agreeable talkers to fill in, and ourselves.

Tuesday

Lady Webster, Mr. Bancroft, and myself, went to Castle Howard, as Lord Morpeth had written to his mother that we were to be there and would lunch with her. Castle Howard is twenty-five miles the other side of York, which is itself twenty-five miles from Newby. But what is fifty miles when one is under the wing of the Railway King and can have a special engine at one's disposal. On arriving at the Castle Howard station we found Lord Carlisle's carriage with four horses and most venerable coachman waiting to receive us. We enter the Park almost immediately, but it is about four miles to the Castle, through many gates, which we had mounted footmen open for us. Lady Carlisle received us in the most delightful manner. . . . I was delighted to see Lord Morpeth's home and his mother, who seldom now goes to London. She was the daughter of the beautiful Duchess of Devonshire, and took me into her own dressing-room to show me her picture. . . . On Wednesday we went into York to witness the reception of Prince Albert, to see the ruins of St. Mary's Abbey, the Flower Show, to lunch with the Lord Mayor, and above all, to attend prayers in the Minister and hear a noble anthem. The Cathedral was crowded with strangers and a great many from London. The next day was the day of the great dinner, and I send you the POST containing Mr. Bancroft's speech. It was warmly admired by all who heard it.

At ten at night we ladies set out for York to go [to] the Lord Mayor's Ball, where the gentlemen were to meet us from the dinner. Everybody flocked round to congratulate me upon your father's speech. Even Prince Albert, when I was led up to make my curtsey, offered me his hand, which is a great courtesy in royalty, and spoke of the great beauty and eloquence of Mr. B.'s speech. The Prince soon went away: the Lord Mayor took me down to supper and I sat between him and the Duke of Richmond at the high table which went across the head of the hall. Guildhall is a beautiful old room with a fine old traceried window, and the scene, with five tables going the length of the hall and the upper one across the head, was very gay and brilliant. There were a few toasts, and your father again made a little speech, short and pleasant. We did not get home till half-past three in the morning. . . . On Friday morning [July 14th] many of the guests, the Duke of Richmond, etc., took their departure and Mr. Hudson had to escort Prince Albert to town, but returned the same evening. . . . The next day we all went to pay a visit to an estate of Mr. Hudson's [name of estate indecipherable] for which he paid five hundred thousand pounds to the Duke of Devonshire. . . . It is nobly situated in the Yorkshire wolds, a fine range of hills, and overlooking the valley of the Humber, which was interesting to me, as it was the river which our Pilgrim fathers sailed down and lay in the Wash at its mouth, awaiting their passage to Holland. They came, our Plymouth fathers, mostly from Lincolnshire and the region which lay below us. I thought of them, and the scene of their sufferings was more ennobled in my eyes, from their remembrance than from the noble mansions and rich estates which feast the eye.

On Monday morning we left Newby for York on our way home. It so happened that the judges were to open the court that very morning, on which occasion they always breakfast with the Lord Mayor in their scarlet robes and wigs, the Lord Mayor and aldermen are also in their furred scarlet robes and the Lady Mayoress presents the judges with enormous bouquets of the richest flowers. We were invited to this breakfast, and I found it very entertaining. I was next the High Sheriff, who was very desirous that we should stay a few hours and go to the castle and see the court opened and listen to a case or two. The High Sheriff of a county is a great character and has a carriage and liveries as grand as the Queen's. After breakfast we bade adieu to our York friends, and set off with our big bouquets (for the distribution was extended to us) for home.

LETTER: To T.D. LONDON, August 9, 1848

My dear Brother: . . . On Saturday we set off for Nuneham, the magnificent seat of the late Archbishop of York, now in possession of his eldest son, Mr. Granville Harcourt. . . . The guests besides ourselves were Sir Robert and Lady Peel, Lord and Lady Villiers, Lord and Lady Norreys, Lord Harry Vane, etc. We considered it a great privilege to be staying in the same house with Sir Robert Peel, and I had also the pleasure of sitting by him at dinner all the three days we were there. He was full of conversation of the best kind. Mr. Denison and Lady Charlotte, his wife, were also of our party. She was the daughter of the Duke of Portland and sister of Lord George Bentinck, Sir Robert's great antagonist in the House.

On Sunday morning we attended the pretty little church on the estate which with its parsonage is a pleasing object on the grounds. The next day the whole party were taken to Blenheim, the seat of the famous Duke of Marlborough, built at the expense of the country. The grounds are exquisite, but I was most charmed by the collection of pictures. Here were the finest Vandykes, Rubens, and Sir Joshua Reynolds which I have seen. Sir Robert Peel is a great connoisseur in art and seemed highly to enjoy them. Altogether it was a truly delightful day: the drive of fifteen miles in open carriages, and through Oxford, being of itself a high pleasure. Yesterday we returned to London, and on Thursday we set out for Scotland.

LETTER: To Mr. and Mrs. I.P.D. EDINBURGH, August 16, 1848

My dear Uncle and Aunt: . . . Of Edinburgh I cannot say enough to express my admiration. The Castle Rock, Arthur's Seat, Salisbury Craigs and Calton Hill are all separate and fine mountains and, with the Frith of Forth, the ocean and the old picturesque town, make an assemblage of fine objects that I have seen nowhere else. Mr. Rutherford, the Lord Advocate, who is of the Ministry, had written to his friends that we were coming, and several gentlemen came by breakfast time the next morning. Mr. Gordon, his nephew, married the daughter of Prof. Wilson, and invited us to dine that day to meet the professor, etc. . . . We drove out after breakfast into the country to Hawthornden, formerly the residence of Drummond the poet, and to Lord Roslin's grounds, where are the ruins of Roslin Castle and above all, of the Roslin Chapel. . . . After lingering and admiring long we returned to Edinburgh just in season for dinner at Mr. Gordon's, where we found Prof. Wilson, and another daughter and son, Mrs. Rutherford, wife of the Lord Advocate, and Capt. Rutherford, his brother, with his wife. We had a very agreeable evening and engaged to dine there again quite EN FAMILLE, with only the professor, whose conversation is delightful.

The next morning we went out to Craigcrook, Lord Jeffrey's country seat, to see and lunch with him. He was confined to his couch. . . . He is seventy-three or seventy-four, but looks not a minute older than fifty. He has a fine head and forehead, and most agreeable and courteous manners, rather of the old school. As he could not rise to receive me he kissed my hand. Mrs. Jeffrey is an intelligent and agreeable woman but has been much out of health the last year. She was Miss Wilkes of New York, you know. The house was an old castellated and fortified house, and with modern additions is a most beautiful residence. Capt. Rutherford told me that when he received the Lord Advocate's letter announcing that we were coming, he went to see Lord Jeffrey to know if he would be well enough to see us, and he expressed the strongest admiration for Mr. Bancroft's work.

This may have disposed them to receive us with the cordiality which made our visit so agreeable. Mr. Empson, his son-in-law and the president editor of the Edinburgh Review, was staying there, and after talking two hours with Lord and Mrs. Jeffrey we took with him a walk in the grounds from which are delightful and commanding views of the whole environs, and never were environs so beautiful.

LETTER: To W.D.B. TARBET ON LOCH LOMOND, August 28, 1848

Dear W. . . . Being detained here by rain this morning I devote it to you and to my journal. . . . The next day was Sunday but the weather being fine we concluded to continue our journey, and followed the Tay seeing Birnam Wood and Dunsinane on our way up to Dunkeld, near to which is the fine seat of the Duke of Athol. We took a delightful walk in the beautiful grounds, and went on to Blair Athol to sleep. This is the chief residence of the Duke of Athol and he has here another house and grounds very pretty though not as extensive as those at Dunkeld. . . . When the innkeeper found who we were he insisted on sending a message to the Duke who sent down an order to us to drive up Glen Tilt and met us there himself. We entered through the Park and followed up the Tilt. Nothing could be more wild than this narrow winding pass which we followed for eight miles till we came to the Duke's forest lodge. Here were waiting for us a most picturesque group in full Highland dress: the head stalker, the head shepherd, the kennel keepers with their dogs in leashes, the piper, etc., etc. They told us that the Duke had sent up word that we were coming and he would soon be there himself.

In a few moments he appeared also in full Highland costume with bare knees, kilt, philibeg, etc. He told us he had then on these mountains 15,000 head of dear, and thought we might like to see a START, as it is called. The head stalker told him, however, that the wind had changed which affects the scent, and that nothing could be done that day. The Duke tried to make us amends by making some of his people sing us Gaelic songs and show us some of the athletic Highland games. The little lodge he also went over with us, and said that the Duchess came there and lived six or seven weeks in the autumn, and that the Duke and Duchess of Buccleuch rented it for many years while he was a minor. If you could see the tiny little rooms, you would be astonished to find what the love of sport can do for these people who possess actual palaces.

After dining again upon salmon and grouse at the pretty little inn, we took a post chaise to go on to Taymouth, a little village adjoining Lord Breadalbane's place. We did not arrive at the inn till after eight and found it completely full. . . . We were sent to the schoolmaster's to sleep in the smallest of little rooms, with a great clock which ticked and struck so loud that we were obliged to silence it, to the great bewilderment, I dare say, of the scholars the next day. Before we were in bed, there was a knock at the door, which proved to be from Lord Breadalbane's butler, to say that he had been commissioned to enquire whenever we arrived at the inn, as his Lordship had heard that we were in Scotland and wished us to make them a visit.

Next morning before we were up came a note from Lord Breadalbane urging us to come immediately to the Castle. . . . Taymouth Castle, though not more than fifty years old, has the air of an old feudal castle. . . . As we were ushered up the magnificent staircase through first a large antechamber, then through a superb hall with lofty ceiling glowing with armorial bearings, and with the most light and delicate carving on every part of the oaken panelling, then through a long gallery, of heavier carving filled with fine old cabinets, into the library, it seemed to me that the whole Castle was one of those magical delusions that one reads of in Fairy Tales, so strange did it seem to find such princely magnificence all alone amid such wild and solitary scenes. I had always the feeling that it would suddenly vanish, at some wave of an enchanter's wand, as it must have arisen also. The library is by far the finest room I ever saw. Its windows and arches and doorways are all of a fine carved Gothic open work as light as gossamer. One door which he lately added cost a thousand pounds, the door alone, not the doorway, so you can judge of the exquisite workmanship. Here Lady Breadalbane joined us, whom I had never before met. . . . During dinner the piper in full costume was playing the pibroch in a gallery outside the window, and after he had done a band, also in full Highland dress, played some of the Italian, German as well as Scotch music, at just an agreeable distance. I have seen nothing in England which compares in splendor with the state which is kept up here.

We passed Wednesday and Thursday here most agreeably, and we rode or walked during the whole days. Lord Breadalbane, by the way, has just been appointed Lord High Chamberlain to the Queen in place of Lord Spencer. I am glad of this because we are brought often in contact with the Lord Chamberlain, but it is very strange to me that a man who lives like a king, and through whose dominions we travelled a hundred miles from the German Ocean to the Atlantic, can be Chamberlain to any Queen. These feudal subordinations we republicans cannot understand. . . . We stopped at the little town of Oban. After reading our letters and getting a dinner, we went out just before sunset for a walk.

We wished much to see the ruins of Dunolly. We passed the porter's lodge and found ourselves directly in the most picturesque grounds on the very shore of the ocean and with the Western Islands lying before us. Mr. Bancroft sent in his card, which brought out instantly the key to the old castle, and in a few moments Capt. MacDougal and Mr. Phipps, a brother of Lord Normanby's, joined us. They pointed out the interesting points in the landscape, the Castle of Ardtornish, the scene of Lord of the Isles, etc., in addition to the fine old ruin we came to see. We lingered till the lighthouses had begun to glow, and I was reminded very much of the scenery at Wood's Hole, which I used to enjoy so much, only that could not boast the association with poetry and feudal romance. We then went into the house, and found a charming domestic circle in full evening dress with short sleeves, so that my gray travelling cloak and straw bonnet were rather out of place. Here were Mrs. Phipps, and Miss Campbell, her sister, daughters of Sir Colin Campbell, and to my great delight, Captain MacDougal brought out the great brooch of Lorn, which his ancestor won from Bruce and the story of which you will find in the Lord of the Isles. It fastened the Scotch Plaid, and is larger than a teacup. He described to me the reverential way in which Scott took it in both hands when he showed it to him. The whole evening was pleasant and the more so from being unexpected. . . . One little thing which adds always to the charm of Scotch scenery is the dress of the peasantry. One never sees the real Highland costume, but every shepherd has his plaid slung over one shoulder, making the most graceful drapery. This, with the universal Glengarry bonnet, is very pretty.

At Glasgow we intended to pay a visit of a day to the historian Alison, but found letters announcing Governor Davis's arrival in London with Mr. Corcoran and immediately turned our faces homeward. We were to have passed a week on our return amidst the lakes, and I protested against going back to London without one look at least. So we stopped at Kendal on Saturday, took a little carriage over to Windermere and Ambleside and passed the whole evening with the poet and Mrs. Wordsworth, at their own exquisite home on Rydal Mount. At ten o'clock we went from there to Miss Martineau, who has built the prettiest of houses in this valley near to Mrs. Arnold at Fox Howe. As we had only one day we made an arrangement with Miss Martineau to go with us and be our guide, and set out the next day at six o'clock and went over to Keswick to breakfast. From thence we went to Borrowdale, by the side of Derwentwater, and afterward to Ulswater and home by the fine pass of Kirkstone. On my return, I found the Duke and Duchess of Argyle had been to see us.

The time of closing the despatch bag has come and I must hurry over my delight at the scenery of the lakes. I could have spent a month there, much to my mind. We arrived home on Monday and early next morning came Mr. Davis and Mr. Corcoran. They went to see the Parliament prorogued in person by the Queen.

LETTER: To Mr. and Mrs. I.P.D. LONDON, December 14, 1848

Dear Uncle and Aunt: On Friday we dined at Mr. Tufnell's, who married last spring the daughter of Lord Rosebery, Lady Anne Primrose, a very "nice person," to use the favorite English term of praise. . . . Sir John Hobhouse was of our party and he told us so much of Byron, who was his intimate friend, as you will remember from his Life, that we stayed much longer than usual at dinner. . . . On Tuesday we were invited to dine with Miss Coutts, but were engaged to Mr. Gurney, an immensely rich Quaker banker, brother of Mrs. Fry. His daughter is married to Ernest Bunsen, the second son of our friend. We were delighted with the whole family scene, which was quite unlike anything we have seen in England. They live at Upton Park, a pretty country seat about eight miles from us, and are surrounded by their children and grandchildren. Their costume and language are strictly Quaker, which was most becoming to Mrs. Gurney's sweet, placid face. . . . Louis Napoleon's election seems fixed, and is to me one of the most astounding things of the age. When we passed several days with him at Mr. Bates's, I would not have given two straws for his chance of a future career. To-night Mendelssohn's "Elijah" is to be performed, and Jenny Lind sings. We had not been able to get tickets, which have been sold for five guineas apiece the last few days. To my great joy Miss Coutts has this moment written me that she has two for our use, and asks us to take an early dinner at five with her and accompany her.

LETTER: To I.P.D. LONDON, June 8, 1849

I thank you, my dear Uncle, for your pleasant letter, which contained as usual much that was interesting to me. And so Mr. and Mrs. Lawrence are to be our successors. . . . Happy as we have been here, I have a great satisfaction that we are setting rather than rising; that we have done our work, instead of having it to do. Like all our pleasures, those here are earned by fatigue and effort, and I would not willingly live the last three years over again, or three years like them, though they have contained high and lasting gratifications. We have constantly the strongest expressions of regret at our approaching departure, and in many cases it is, I know, most genuine. My relations here have been most agreeable, and particularly in that intellectual circle whose high character and culture have made their regard most precious to me. The manifestations of this kindness increase as the time approaches for our going and we are inundated with invitations of all kinds.

Young Prescott is here. I wish Prescott could have seen his reception at Lady Lovelace's the other evening when there happened to be a collection of genius and literature. What a blessing it is SOMETIMES to a son to have a father.

To-morrow we dine with Lord John Russell down at Pembroke Lodge in Richmond Park. On Monday we breakfast with Macaulay. We met him at dinner this week at Lady Waldegrave's, and he said: "Would you be willing to breakfast with me some morning, if I asked one or two other ladies?" "Willing!" I said, "I should be delighted beyond measure." So he sent us a note for Monday next. I depend upon seeing his bachelor establishment, his library, and mode of life. On Wednesday we go to a ball at the Palace. But it is useless to go on, for every day is filled in this way, and gives you an idea of London in the season.

LETTER: To I.P.D. LONDON, June 22, 1849

My dear Uncle: Yesterday I passed one of the most agreeable days I have had in England at Oxford, where I went with a party to see Mr. Bancroft take his degree. . . . Nothing could have gone off better than the whole thing. Mr. Bancroft went up the day before, but Mrs. Stuart Mackenzie and her daughter, with Lady Elizabeth Waldegrave, Louisa, and myself went up yesterday morning and returned at night. We lunched at the Vice-Chancellor's (where Mr. B. made a pleasant little informal speech) and were treated with great kindness by everybody. I wish you could have seen Mr. Bancroft walking round all day with his scarlet gown and round velvet cap, such as you see in old Venetian pictures. From this time forward we shall have the pain of bidding adieu, one by one, to our friends, as they leave town not to return till we are gone.

www.bookjungle.com *email: sales@bookjungle.com fax: 630-214-0564 mail: Book Jungle PO Box 2226 Champaign, IL 61825*

The Codes Of Hammurabi And Moses
W. W. Davies

QTY

The discovery of the Hammurabi Code is one of the greatest achievements of archaeology, and is of paramount interest, not only to the student of the Bible, but also to all those interested in ancient history...

Religion   **ISBN:** *1-59462-338-4*   **Pages:132**
MSRP $12.95

The Theory of Moral Sentiments
Adam Smith

QTY

This work from 1749. contains original theories of conscience amd moral judgment and it is the foundation for systemof morals.

Philosophy **ISBN:** *1-59462-777-0*   **Pages:536**
MSRP $19.95

Jessica's First Prayer
Hesba Stretton

QTY

In a screened and secluded corner of one of the many railway-bridges which span the streets of London there could be seen a few years ago, from five o'clock every morning until half past eight, a tidily set-out coffee-stall, consisting of a trestle and board, upon which stood two large tin cans, with a small fire of charcoal burning under each so as to keep the coffee boiling during the early hours of the morning when the work-people were thronging into the city on their way to their daily toil...

Pages:84

Childrens **ISBN:** *1-59462-373-2*   *MSRP $9.95*

My Life and Work
Henry Ford

QTY

Henry Ford revolutionized the world with his implementation of mass production for the Model T automobile. Gain valuable business insight into his life and work with his own auto-biography... "We have only started on our development of our country we have not as yet, with all our talk of wonderful progress, done more than scratch the surface. The progress has been wonderful enough but..."

Pages:300

Biographies/   **ISBN:** *1-59462-198-5*   *MSRP $21.95*

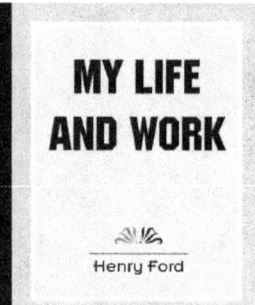

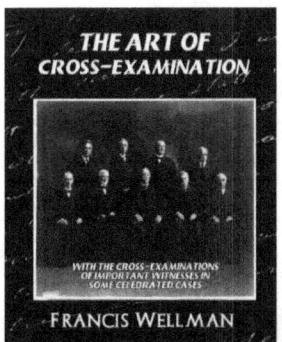

The Art of Cross-Examination
Francis Wellman

QTY

I presume it is the experience of every author, after his first book is published upon an important subject, to be almost overwhelmed with a wealth of ideas and illustrations which could readily have been included in his book, and which to his own mind, at least, seem to make a second edition inevitable. Such certainly was the case with me; and when the first edition had reached its sixth impression in five months, I rejoiced to learn that it seemed to my publishers that the book had met with a sufficiently favorable reception to justify a second and considerably enlarged edition. ..

Pages:412

Reference   ISBN: *1-59462-647-2*   *MSRP $19.95*

On the Duty of Civil Disobedience
Henry David Thoreau

QTY

Thoreau wrote his famous essay, On the Duty of Civil Disobedience, as a protest against an unjust but popular war and the immoral but popular institution of slave-owning. He did more than write—he declined to pay his taxes, and was hauled off to gaol in consequence. Who can say how much this refusal of his hastened the end of the war and of slavery ?

Law   ISBN: *1-59462-747-9*

Pages:48

MSRP $7.45

Dream Psychology Psychoanalysis for Beginners
Sigmund Freud

QTY

Sigmund Freud, born Sigismund Schlomo Freud (May 6, 1856 - September 23, 1939), was a Jewish-Austrian neurologist and psychiatrist who co-founded the psychoanalytic school of psychology. Freud is best known for his theories of the unconscious mind, especially involving the mechanism of repression; his redefinition of sexual desire as mobile and directed towards a wide variety of objects; and his therapeutic techniques, especially his understanding of transference in the therapeutic relationship and the presumed value of dreams as sources of insight into unconscious desires.

Pages:196

Psychology   ISBN: *1-59462-905-6*   *MSRP $15.45*

The Miracle of Right Thought
Orison Swett Marden

QTY

Believe with all of your heart that you will do what you were made to do. When the mind has once formed the habit of holding cheerful, happy, prosperous pictures, it will not be easy to form the opposite habit. It does not matter how improbable or how far away this realization may see, or how dark the prospects may be, if we visualize them as best we can, as vividly as possible, hold tenaciously to them and vigorously struggle to attain them, they will gradually become actualized, realized in the life. But a desire, a longing without endeavor, a yearning abandoned or held indifferently will vanish without realization.

Pages:360

Self Help   ISBN: *1-59462-644-8*   *MSRP $25.45*

The Rosicrucian Cosmo-Conception Mystic Christianity *by Max Heindel*   ISBN: *1-59462-188-8*   **$38.95**
The Rosicrucian Cosmo-conception is not dogmatic, neither does it appeal to any other authority than the reason of the student. It is: not controversial, but is: sent forth in the, hope that it may help to clear...
New Age/Religion Pages 646

Abandonment To Divine Providence *by Jean-Pierre de Caussade*   ISBN: *1-59462-228-0*   **$25.95**
"The Rev. Jean Pierre de Caussade was one of the most remarkable spiritual writers of the Society of Jesus in France in the 18th Century. His death took place at Toulouse in 1751. His works have gone through many editions and have been republished...
Inspirational/Religion Pages 400

Mental Chemistry *by Charles Haanel*   ISBN: *1-59462-192-6*   **$23.95**
Mental Chemistry allows the change of material conditions by combining and appropriately utilizing the power of the mind. Much like applied chemistry creates something new and unique out of careful combinations of chemicals the mastery of mental chemistry...
New Age Pages 354

The Letters of Robert Browning and Elizabeth Barret Barrett 1845-1846 vol II   ISBN: *1-59462-193-4*   **$35.95**
by Robert Browning and Elizabeth Barrett
Biographies Pages 596

Gleanings In Genesis (volume I) *by Arthur W. Pink*   ISBN: *1-59462-130-6*   **$27.45**
Appropriately has Genesis been termed "the seed plot of the Bible" for in it we have, in germ form, almost all of the great doctrines which are afterwards fully developed in the books of Scripture which follow...
Religion/Inspirational Pages 420

The Master Key *by L. W. de Laurence*   ISBN: *1-59462-001-6*   **$30.95**
In no branch of human knowledge has there been a more lively increase of the spirit of research during the past few years than in the study of Psychology, Concentration and Mental Discipline. The requests for authentic lessons in Thought Control, Mental Discipline and...
New Age/Business Pages 422

The Lesser Key Of Solomon Goetia *by L. W. de Laurence*   ISBN: *1-59462-092-X*   **$9.95**
This translation of the first book of the "Lernegton" which is now for the first time made accessible to students of Talismanic Magic was done, after careful collation and edition, from numerous Ancient Manuscripts in Hebrew, Latin, and French...
New Age/Occult Pages 92

Rubaiyat Of Omar Khayyam *by Edward Fitzgerald*   ISBN:*1-59462-332-5*   **$13.95**
Edward Fitzgerald, whom the world has already learned, in spite of his own efforts to remain within the shadow of anonymity, to look upon as one of the rarest poets of the century, was born at Bredfield, in Suffolk, on the 31st of March, 1809. He was the third son of John Purcell...
Music Pages 172

Ancient Law *by Henry Maine*   ISBN: *1-59462-128-4*   **$29.95**
The chief object of the following pages is to indicate some of the earliest ideas of mankind, as they are reflected in Ancient Law, and to point out the relation of those ideas to modern thought.
Religion/History Pages 452

Far-Away Stories *by William J. Locke*   ISBN: *1-59462-129-2*   **$19.45**
"Good wine needs no bush, but a collection of mixed vintages does. And this book is just such a collection. Some of the stories I do not want to remain buried for ever in the museum files of dead magazine-numbers an author's not unpardonable vanity..."
Fiction Pages 272

Life of David Crockett *by David Crockett*   ISBN: *1-59462-250-7*   **$27.45**
"Colonel David Crockett was one of the most remarkable men of the times in which he lived. Born in humble life, but gifted with a strong will, an indomitable courage, and unremitting perseverance...
Biographies/New Age Pages 424

Lip-Reading *by Edward Nitchie*   ISBN: *1-59462-206-X*   **$25.95**
Edward B. Nitchie, founder of the New York School for the Hard of Hearing, now the Nitchie School of Lip-Reading, Inc, wrote "LIP-READING Principles and Practice". The development and perfecting of this meritorious work on lip-reading was an undertaking...
How-to Pages 400

A Handbook of Suggestive Therapeutics, Applied Hypnotism, Psychic Science   ISBN: *1-59462-214-0*   **$24.95**
by Henry Munro
Health/New Age/Health/Self-help Pages 376

A Doll's House: and Two Other Plays *by Henrik Ibsen*   ISBN: *1-59462-112-8*   **$19.95**
Henrik Ibsen created this classic when in revolutionary 1848 Rome. Introducing some striking concepts in playwriting for the realist genre, this play has been studied the world over.
Fiction/Classics/Plays 308

The Light of Asia *by sir Edwin Arnold*   ISBN: *1-59462-204-3*   **$13.95**
In this poetic masterpiece, Edwin Arnold describes the life and teachings of Buddha. The man who was to become known as Buddha to the world was born as Prince Gautama of India but he rejected the worldly riches and abandoned the reigns of power when...
Religion/History/Biographies Pages 170

The Complete Works of Guy de Maupassant *by Guy de Maupassant*   ISBN: *1-59462-157-8*   **$16.95**
"For days and days, nights and nights, I had dreamed of that first kiss which was to consecrate our engagement, and I knew not on what spot I should put my lips..."
Fiction/Classics Pages 240

The Art of Cross-Examination *by Francis L. Wellman*   ISBN: *1-59462-309-0*   **$26.95**
Written by a renowned trial lawyer, Wellman imparts his experience and uses case studies to explain how to use psychology to extract desired information through questioning.
How-to/Science/Reference Pages 408

Answered or Unanswered? *by Louisa Vaughan*   ISBN: *1-59462-248-5*   **$10.95**
Miracles of Faith in China
Religion Pages 112

The Edinburgh Lectures on Mental Science (1909) *by Thomas*   ISBN: *1-59462-008-3*   **$11.95**
This book contains the substance of a course of lectures recently given by the writer in the Queen Street Hall, Edinburgh. Its purpose is to indicate the Natural Principles governing the relation between Mental Action and Material Conditions...
New Age/Psychology Pages 148

Ayesha *by H. Rider Haggard*   ISBN: *1-59462-301-5*   **$24.95**
Verily and indeed it is the unexpected that happens! Probably if there was one person upon the earth from whom the Editor of this, and of a certain previous history, did not expect to hear again...
Classics Pages 380

Ayala's Angel *by Anthony Trollope*   ISBN: *1-59462-352-X*   **$29.95**
The two girls were both pretty, but Lucy who was twenty-one who supposed to be simple and comparatively unattractive, whereas Ayala was credited, as her Bombwhat romantic would show, with poetic charm and a taste for romance. Ayala when her father died was nineteen...
Fiction Pages 484

The American Commonwealth *by James Bryce*   ISBN: *1-59462-286-8*   **$34.45**
An interpretation of American democratic political theory. It examines political mechanics and society from the perspective of Scotsman James Bryce
Politics Pages 572

Stories of the Pilgrims *by Margaret P. Pumphrey*   ISBN: *1-59462-116-0*   **$17.95**
This book explores pilgrims religious oppression in England as well as their escape to Holland and eventual crossing to America on the Mayflower, and their early days in New England...
History Pages 268

QTY

The Fasting Cure *by Sinclair Upton*   ISBN: *1-59462-222-1* **$13.95**
In the Cosmopolitan Magazine for May, 1910, and in the Contemporary Review (London) for April, 1910, I published an article dealing with my experiences in fasting. I have written a great many magazine articles, but never one which attracted so much attention... New Age/Self Help/Health Pages 164

Hebrew Astrology *by Sepharial*   ISBN: *1-59462-308-2* **$13.45**
In these days of advanced thinking it is a matter of common observation that we have left many of the old landmarks behind and that we are now pressing forward to greater heights and to a wider horizon than that which represented the mind-content of our progenitors... Astrology Pages 144

Thought Vibration or The Law of Attraction in the Thought World   ISBN: *1-59462-127-6* **$12.95**

by William Walker Atkinson   *Psychology/Religion Pages 144*

Optimism *by Helen Keller*   ISBN: *1-59462-108-X* **$15.95**
Helen Keller was blind, deaf, and mute since 19 months old, yet famously learned how to overcome these handicaps, communicate with the world, and spread her lectures promoting optimism. An inspiring read for everyone... Biographies/Inspirational Pages 84

Sara Crewe *by Frances Burnett*   ISBN: *1-59462-360-0* **$9.45**
In the first place, Miss Minchin lived in London. Her home was a large, dull, tall one, in a large, dull square, where all the houses were alike, and all the sparrows were alike, and where all the door-knockers made the same heavy sound... Childrens/Classic Pages 88

The Autobiography of Benjamin Franklin *by Benjamin Franklin*   ISBN: *1-59462-135-7* **$24.95**
The Autobiography of Benjamin Franklin has probably been more extensively read than any other American historical work, and no other book of its kind has had such ups and downs of fortune. Franklin lived for many years in England, where he was agent... Biographies/History Pages 332

Name	
Email	
Telephone	
Address	
City, State ZIP	

☐ **Credit Card**   ☐ **Check / Money Order**

Credit Card Number	
Expiration Date	
Signature	

Please Mail to: Book Jungle
PO Box 2226
Champaign, IL 61825
or Fax to: 630-214-0564

ORDERING INFORMATION

web: *www.bookjungle.com*
email: *sales@bookjungle.com*
fax: *630-214-0564*
mail: *Book Jungle PO Box 2226 Champaign, IL 61825*
or PayPal *to sales@bookjungle.com*

Please contact us for bulk discounts

DIRECT-ORDER TERMS

**20% Discount if You Order
Two or More Books**
Free Domestic Shipping!
Accepted: Master Card, Visa,
Discover, American Express